NO PULLING BACK

NO PULLING BACK
(TALE OF A FIGHTER DOG)

Ruth Ann Hanley

 INFINITY
PUBLISHING

ISBN 978-0-7414-8218-1 Paperback
ISBN 978-0-7414-8219-8 eBook

Printed in the United States of America

Published September 2013; 2nd Edition April 2015

INFINITY PUBLISHING
1094 New DeHaven Street, Suite 100
West Conshohocken, PA 19428-2713
Toll-free (877) BUY BOOK
Local Phone (610) 941-9999
Fax (610) 941-9959
Info@buybooksontheweb.com
www.buybooksontheweb.com

Dedicated to Mary, the best mother of all

And to my many helpers who showed the same goodness
and generosity that appealed to this fighter dog

CONTENTS

CHAPTER I

Daemon

He had not eaten in thirty-six hours, through night, day and night. He lay outstretched on the river bank, feeling the strands of grass and tiny stones against his belly. His strong pulling muscles, even when relaxed, betrayed the hard physical life to which he was accustomed. Muscles so hard that even the small stones among the grasses were unable to imbed themselves. He had slept for twelve hours, exhausted. His head ached where the boat's prow had fallen against it. His memory of what and how it had happened was vague, coming back in disjointed pictures, like sand particles, each distinct, but scattered loosely.

His partner was gone. He knew that. At the time of the accident, when the boat had overturned and the prow had hit Daemon in the head above his right eye, he had lost consciousness for a few moments and been separated from Taursus. After struggling to the bank, vomiting water into the sand and falling into his discharge, Daemon looked for him. Where was he? He was not on the bank. Was he in the water? He had played so many tricks on Daemon, called him "dumb" so many times, that Daemon could have believed another trick. Yet, this time he was not to be fooled.

He plunged back into the swollen, raging waters to search. Until nightfall he battled debris crashing down the river and got pounded until his body throbbed. Still he searched . . . until he was engulfed and dragged under water by the dangling branch of a large tree that rolled down the river. Under water his limbs flailed up and down, right and left. They were uncontrollable. Panic took him as he swallowed a huge mouthful of water. Then, just as quickly as it had taken him under, the tree shot him back to the surface. There, with strength born of terror, he struggled free and back to shore.

Safely there, he now knew he would not go in again. Taursus could save himself.

Taursus was strong. He was a soldier. He led the way and for two years Daemon followed him without complaint. Daemon had been trained to follow orders. He had learned to kill on command. He followed one man and one man alone, but he never freely submitted to him. He would rather die than that.

Daemon was strong too. Before he partnered with Taursus he worked the Roman amphitheater. Though he had no given name, he was known by his handlers as "Short Ear," "Auris Brevis," because of a clumsy crop that left one ear slightly shorter than the other. But he had no deficiencies as a fighter. He would go out with three other fighter dogs, following a hunter with his whip and sword as the music began.

Far off in the amphitheater would be a huge brown animal, scared, angry and foaming at the mouth. They called it a bear, "Ursus." At the command of the hunter they would advance on this animal like a swarm of angry hornets. The animal, standing upright, would slash with its paws and often disembowel the first to come in close. But while the slasher was having his way with that one, Daemon would attack from the rear. Standing squarely on his thick strong legs which were slightly bowed, with his large feet, making no noise whatsoever and unlike his companions who were screaming in rage and fear, he would advance swiftly. While his bloodied companion was screaming in a death agony he would slide behind the large animal and deal a slashing attack at its leg tendons. Then just as swiftly he would bow low to the ground and away in order to miss the now cataclysmic anger, rage and savage swings of club-like paws.

Fighters and animal alike would soon be sprinkled with blood, and the ground would be slippery with blood and the entrails of the young fighter who had his first bout in the amphitheater . . . and his last. The bear would continue charging but would be hindered by his weakened legs. Slowly and methodically, one by one, the fighters would tear wounds into him. The dispatch lasted a long time and the people in the stands yelled gleefully when another fighter was wounded. Daemon sensed that they wanted the killing to last. And so, he himself usually stood back allowing the others to continue the slaughter. Always, at the end the hunter would rush in sword first and slide his weapon into the weakened animal, now prostrate on the ground. When the hunter acted, all the fighters were to draw back. This was supposed to be the hunter's triumph. In fact, because they were so wrought up, the fighters often wanted to finish the kill themselves but they would be whipped back by slaves and made to return instead to their cages under the amphitheater.

3

The last time Daemon was in the amphitheater that hunter made a huge mistake. He had stabbed the animal, but missed a vital spot, allowing the animal to fake its death. When the bear fell, the slaves came to whip the fighter dogs back to their cages. But Daemon broke away from the other snarling, yet controlled, fighters. He sensed what was happening. To get by the nearest slave he whirled and ran close to that one's body and under his extended arm. With a futile swipe his whip cracked the empty air. Nonetheless, Daemon was too late. As the hunter turned his back to the animal to bow to the crowd for his crown of glory leaves, the animal grabbed him from behind, hugging him down upon its chest with its bloody paws.

Daemon ran to the throbbing, blood-spurting pair locked in an embrace on the amphitheater floor. In a warm rush the smell of fear enveloped him from both bodies. Tucking his legs under him, he vaulted over the hunter's broad sword which lay a man's distance from the bloody mound. The hunter's eyes were as wide with terror as the bear's. Daemon rushed to the bear and clamped onto its throat as best he could for it was huge and slippery. As he held and shook it, the bear and hunter joined in an eerie death rattle, composed of groan and then sharp counterpoint. He held on as hard as he could, shaking until his teeth hurt, concerned that he would slide off, and like the hunter, not succeed with his kill. He reveled in their fear smell and the fresh blood now pouring out. The blood spattered his face and chest as he shook. He held on until his victim gurgled a death rattle and then let go of the hunter with a powerful shudder. The release was, of course, too late for the man.

Then Daemon went wild in triumph. He bit the animal on the face, shredding its nose, then pulled out its tongue

4

which was lolling to the side. He bit that off also and tossed it to the floor amid the already sun-warmed animal parts. The animal's body shifted and its huge, heavy paws slid sideways, almost knocking Daemon from his perch. His large feet slid in the gore as he systematically attacked the ears from behind, holding one up like a trophy before he tossed it aside and grabbed for the second.

The crowd was ecstatic. Never had it been treated to such a display of wanton destruction. It yelled him on. "Go, go, go . . ." People standing in the stands. Others trying to even climb over the stands to engage in the bloody gore on the field. Some parents with young children went the opposite way, sensing full-blown chaos and wanting to get out without getting knocked down and stepped upon. They screamed too, but in fear, as they pushed their children through the crowd which was advancing toward the mound of hunter, bear and fighter dog.

A slave came to chase Daemon off the kill, but Daemon turned and stood his ground. He would rather quarrel than yield. When the whip slashed his face and cut across the bridge of his nose, the crowd booed its displeasure at the man who tried to bring order. For the first time in all his amphitheater bouts Daemon had been striped by a whip. He wore his own blood, mingled with that of the animals spread about him. He glared at the slave. Atop the mountain of dead animal and dead human Daemon drew a deep penetrating growl from the depths of his being. The stands quieted. The deep guttural sound rolled on. It did not come in single breaths. It did not lessen, but seemed to get louder and louder. And it shocked the stands into silence. The slave turned and ran.

Those few men who had climbed down the walls and into the amphitheater, beat a hasty retreat, leaving a pile of dust, a sandal and small dagger near the stands. Slaves with whips had had no trouble driving the other fighter dogs back under the stands. Eagerly, almost knocking each other down, they had run to the cages set out for them, their tails between their legs.

Daemon ignored the dogs and the slaves. This was his kill. He had played by the rules but the men had not. The growl continued. It was his tribute to himself. He had no concern for his three companions now caged. Nor did he advance on the second man coming at him with a whip, but that fellow hesitated; then dropping the whip, he ran for help, his tunic flapping in the breeze, his boney knees knocking together.

Next came three more huge slave volunteers, fighting, perhaps for their freedom. Sometimes if a slave succeeded in the amphitheater he was given freedom. This seemed like a task which might bring such a reward. These men were also those whose lives could be lost without public or private mourning. Not like a famed or favorite hunter of the crowd. They carried spears and it was obvious that they were sent to dispatch Daemon as he sat upon the mountainous, bloody and disfigured heap, growling deep and guttural.

But now an animal-like shouting of indistinguishable sounds and growls came from the crowd. It rose in anger against the slaves. Like an advancing war-ready cohort, it grew louder and angrier in an attempt to prevent the slaughter of Daemon. Never had the crowd seen a fighter like Daemon, one who would not be cowed by the slaves nor the bear. Never had one of the fighters stood his ground against such a large animal as well as against those in charge. Never had such a contest taken a turn like this. As the tallest slave who had a scar across his face where he too had been slashed by a whip, raised his spear to hurl it at Daemon, the crowd stood as one, with thumbs up meaning to spare Daemon. It booed even more loudly at the slave and began hurling drinking cups and shoes, and whatever else was available, at the three sent to dispatch the fighter dog.

When the slaves backed off, the crowd cheered. Daemon only knew that he was allowed to continue his attack on the dead bear. When the crowd finally became bored and distracted, a slave, a former fisherman, came out with a folded net rimmed with many small weights. From a distance he tossed it over the heap. As it rose it spread. It descended as a perfect circle to cover Daemon, the bear and the hunter. Slaves then removed the dead young fighter dog and cleaned up the bloody bear parts. With strong horses they dragged their netted catch into the area under the amphitheater. Everything under there smelled of death. The fighter who had been gored by the bear was heaped into an urn with its grey wolf-like tail hanging out and down the side. The dead hunter was pulled by one broken leg from under the net. Broken ribs pierced his chest like jagged sticks. They put him on a cot behind the fighter dog cages. Daemon had only disdain for them both. Neither was a good fighter and neither would fight again.

Daemon was puzzled by the feeling under the stands. Whereas the outside crowd had loved his savage attacks and his refusal to return to his cage, inside, under the amphitheater, he sensed no approval from those in charge. Thus, even though the crowd loved Daemon, he sensed this was his last bout in the amphitheater. This was the last time the flowers and cheers would rain on him. He had once been starved almost unto death to prepare him for a match in the amphitheater, and he had no affection for those who starved him. The only time he felt connected to them was when they reveled with him as he scared, ripped and killed. His memory ran a tape of his kills as he lay under the bloody net: bulls, bear, rhinoceros, elephant, rams, humans.

Today, however, after this contest, he sensed a new emotion under this amphitheater which he had never felt after a fight: fear towards him from those in charge. All of these humans who had formerly respected him and given him space, now were sweating and their glands emitting a cloud of fear such as he usually only smelled from those he was ordered to kill. He could sense that he could not live among these any more. He would either be their master or be destroyed. They could not remain living side by side. He sensed now from this fear that the plan had changed from a plan to use him as a draw for the crowd to a plan to dispatch him out of sight of the crowd. He knew this from their smell and looks. They looked at him the way they looked at the animals to be killed. They retained respect for his ferocious nature, but they were unwilling to work with him. They did not want that type of challenge. Would they send in the other fighter dogs to dispatch him? He hoped so. He was eager to fight them. He was not afraid. Not even of all of them together. He had only disdain for the humans and the fighter dogs.

However, under the amphitheater there was no time for a gang execution. The amphitheater crowd was waiting. The next large animal was already out there. The music sounded and a hunter marched past Daemon, stepping on the edge of the covering net. As he passed, an Editor, who tended the area under the amphitheater, backed away to make room for the fresh fighter dogs and a strong dark-skinned slave leaving the amphitheater. It was their turn to kill, and the fickle crowd would never know or care what happened to Daemon.

That was a false hope: that Daemon would be forgotten. Already out in the amphitheater someone had drawn Daemon's picture on a white cloak: a large one-hundred-forty-pound canine. His eyes were yellowish. His nostrils evenly spaced. He had a large blocky head. His lips pulled back to reveal two projecting fangs, sharp and glistening. He had cropped ears and the careful artist noted and drew the one slightly shorter than the other. His hair was medium length, thick and coarse. His shoulders and neck were thick and muscular. He had long thighs and shanks and was of a metallic black color laced with tan. He was formidable and of all the animals one could meet after dark, the least desirable. The artist held up his picture of the big dog and the crowd cheered again. Under the picture he had written one word: DAEMON. It was surrounded by specks and splatters of red.

When the Editor heard the cheering, he looked out and caught a glimpse of the drawing. What he saw made him tremble. He now hesitated to use the large spear on the dog glaring at him from under the net. The politics of the amphitheater made it seem possible to him that he could be blamed for the death of this fighter dog so beloved of the crowd. He might bear the blame, not his superiors. He could see himself as bait for the lions and large cats. His death would expiate the crowd's anger for the dispatch of the dog. He was certainly not willing to be a sin offering, a phrase he had taken from an angry Israeli prisoner as he

9

was marched under guard into the amphitheater. On the other hand, the Editor could never again use this dog in the amphitheater. He could not be trusted. The Editor would be blamed if Daemon turned on his handlers, if he attacked the wrong person.

So he left Daemon under the net.

A light breeze stirred the net. It came from the amphitheater together with muffled growls and yelps of pain. Daemon knew at what stage the amphitheater battle raged. He knew the large animal was still in charge. Two fighter dogs had been downed. He heard their death moans. He watched the backs of the slaves standing at the entrance to the amphitheater. They ignored him now. But they were sweating even though it was past the heat of the day.

Finally a triumphant roar came from the crowd. The slaves ran forward. At the Editor's signal five more slaves joined in the rush. Daemon knew that the animal had caught the hunter. The crowd was still in a spiteful mood. He could feel its wish to inflict harm on another human. Then it came: a second win for a large animal because the slaves came too late. Before they could stop the carnage, the victim screamed a sharp, staccato note, then gurgled his surrender, barely audible to the dogs under the amphitheater. Yet they were up from their resting spots and scratching at the doors of their cages. Whining a "let me out." They were let out. And despite their many wounds from the previous fight they used every ounce of energy, knocking each other aside as they raced and limped through the doorway. Daemon knew the sounds as they piled onto the large animal. And soon that animal screeched his own death yell.

Not all the fighter dogs returned to their cages. Two of them were dumped into urns, overfilling them. And the blood ran down the sides and pooled on the floor until it trickled into Daemon's net. He licked it up. He was full from the bear parts he had ingested, but he had learned to eat as much as possible against the time that he would be starved for another fight.

Now the outside stands were thinning. Daemon could hear from the voices that they were moving farther and farther away. Daemon realized the last fight was over. Two humans had been dispatched, two large animals and three fighter dogs. Daemon felt no remorse, not even for the fighter dogs. The only remorse was that he had not been in on the second kill. They had not lifted the net and allowed him into the amphitheater to bite and gouge and rip.

Two horse carts drew up to the doorway. He watched the slaves lift the dog cages into the carts and pull away. They took all the fighter dogs but him. Still Daemon did not whine. He did not growl. He lay silent on the dirt floor . . . But he was vigilant as a snake waiting to strike.

.

CHAPTER II

Rescue

Footsteps came near. He could tell it was a Roman soldier by the slap of the leather boots on the floor. The man tripped over the edge of the net and fell beside Daemon. His knee rested on Daemon's leg. But Daemon did not strike though his hackles rose. Those short coarse hackles puffed up like troops, aching for a fight. The man swore an oath and rubbed his knee. Then he laughed, a long hard laugh. That laugh came from a flat face rippled with scars, coarse and darkened by the sun.

"You're just what I was looking for," he grinned at the dog. "You are tough as nails. You are not afraid of me and I'm not afraid of you. You are vicious and wicked, just like me. You will get a lot of respect from those damned Israelis in Jerusalem. They are as stubborn as you are, but you have those wonderful, ripping teeth."

"What do you think you are doing?" came the loud accusation from behind the soldier. Taursus whirled.

"Who do you think you are to come at a soldier this way?" he retorted smoothly, in a tone fit for an investigator in a torture chamber.

The accuser was visibly shaken. It had been a terrible day and he still had not solved the problem of what to do about the uncontrollable dog. "Sorry sir, in this dim light I did not see your rank. How can I help you?" he groveled as if it were an everyday occurrence to find a soldier down beside a bloody, netted dog.

"I'm thinking of taking this problem off your hands," Taursus answered smoothly. "I go into battle, or at least into enemy territory next week. I'll have this big, scary son of Zeus with me. He'll get me some respect."

"I need to tell you, sir, that he is uncontrollable," the Editor whimpered. He certainly did not want to be responsible for this stupid man's death by dog attack. Had he been in the amphitheater? Had he seen what happened today: the wanton disobedience? "Were you in the amphitheater today? Did you see that he would not back off when ordered?"

Taursus stood. With the back of his hand he struck the Editor a blow across his face. The blow was hard enough to twist his neck and knock him to his knees.

Though he had not seen it, the blow reverberated in Daemon. He raised his head, pushing part of the heavy net upward. His own neck echoed the site of that painful jarring as a few inches above the victim's shoulder. He had learned to tune into the slightest change in a victim, to pinpoint every weakness. A master tool in a fight.

"Never mind the dog," Taursus yelled. "Your manners are scarcely better. Bring me a stout rope and tie another high to the flag pole."

14

The Editor, who managed the pace and order of the bouts, did as he was told. He realized that now the amphitheater was almost empty. Nobody was there to help him. He might die in the amphitheater for giving this soldier the dog, but he might die quicker by refusing to do as ordered.

"Please, sir," he pleaded, "what will I tell the audience at the next display? They want this dog to perform for them."

Ignoring the question and briskly reaching under the net, Taursus grabbed Daemon's left back leg and tied it with the rope. Daemon snarled and tried to reach him, but only grabbed a mouthful of net. Next Taursus stepped on the rope, and folding part of the net, he secured the second fighting and kicking back limb to the first.

Daemon had never been treated this way. He needed his large muscular feet to push himself forward in an attack. With open mouth and lip pulled back he waited for his chance. There would be no pulling back. This would be a kill.

Taursus was in no hurry. He moved deliberately just as Daemon always did. Daemon felt his feet jerked up so that he was lifted into the air, net hanging and scraping the floor. Next Taursus ripped the net off his body.

Daemon saw Taursus back off and look at him with a smile. He could tell the man was pleased. Could Daemon swing close enough to grab him? Daemon started pumping his front legs, but all that he succeeded in doing was swinging in small erratic circles. Then he felt a whack on his back sending him into a larger circle. Soon he was spinning round and round into faster and faster circles. He felt each whack on his ribs and back. These hits were not as damaging as when he got stomped by his first bull. But they were deliberate and strong. Soon Daemon was concentrating on pulling his front legs together. He was no longer snarling. The spinning went on for a long time. It was dark now and the Editor brought a burning branch and set it in a holder close by.

Finally Daemon felt his body swiftly descend and land with a heavy thump. Before he could get his breath and his front legs under him he felt a strong knee in his shoulder, pushing downward, and an iron-like grasp on his throat to the side and under his jaw. He struggled to get up from under this burden. As he did he felt the knee push deeper, the grasp on his throat tighten. He was not afraid to die, but after struggling with every muscle in his body and trying to throw off the attacker, he became curious as to this human, the first who did not run from his snarling, foaming face. This man was the first who did not emit a cloud of rancid, full-blown fear. Daemon could not have explained it. He had never in his life given in to an opponent. He had never before surrendered. But now he lay still. It was the smart thing to do. Someday he would get an opportunity to fight back.

Taursus removed a strip of dried animal skin from around his stout middle. Daemon watched silently and remained still as Taursus lifted his head slightly and slid it under. He felt the pressure around his strong muscular neck as the dried skin encircled it. It was like a huge hand that applied pressure from more than one direction. It smelled too of a sharp, pungent material like a cleaner used on the amphitheater floor. He identified the source animal as a fairly young one, likely to have been chased down and speared by soldiers. Taursus pulled the skin out part way and stabbed a hole into it with his sword and fastened it.

"Come, Daemon," Taursus laughed. He jerked on the skin and Daemon rose quickly as he felt its tug at his throat. He was eager to leave the amphitheater, eager to go to the kennels and wait for the next fight. But instead of walking toward the kennels Taursus walked out past them and into the darkness with Daemon following.

Daemon soon learned his new trade. Taursus took back his leather bound and put it around his own middle. Instead Daemon was given an even stronger circular neck bound made out of the same material as the weapon worn by Taursus. It was solid metal. It snapped together and had spikes that would be disaster to any attacking enemy which grabbed his throat. Now it hurt his own foot to scratch his neck. His foot came away bloody. So he stopped scratching.

Taursus worked with him every afternoon in a field not far from the amphitheater. He soon learned not to stop and eat any dead animals. He learned not to roll into dung or decaying animals. That was the hardest lesson, engrained into him by a second tying and lifting and spinning. It had always been his favorite sport. He would plunge his upper neck and right ear into the pile and burrow with his shoulder. He carried the slimy patch proudly. Any time he wanted he could inhale and enjoy its fullness. Now he was denied those full rich smells. He was not even permitted to get close to dogs or humans that they met . . . unless Taursus released him. Now at least he had a name, the one the crowd had given him and which richly suited him: "Daemon." When he heard it, he put it into his memory and stacked up each repeated

17

calling of it and thus practiced it until he knew it. Now it was in his memory bank.

That release from the amphitheater was glorious. After a few weeks Taursus did not cage him nor even tie him, but held him with his voice. Daemon learned quickly, stacking the meaningful words and gestures upon each other until he recognized them all. His small inside-the-head dictionary held "Daemon," "stay," "come," "eat," "back" and "kill." Finding a pack of loose dogs toward evening, Taursus would yell "KILL" and Daemon would be off. At first they would surround him to fight, but soon, and especially if he cut one out and disemboweled it, the others would run from him into the darkness, yipping and screaming. His secret was to attack low, to bend his legs and throw himself onto one of them. The others could not get low enough to attack his legs. Once a wolfish-looking runt got his tail, but Daemon was three times heavier and he whirled so fast that he threw the attacker into another with a hard crack. Then he finished them both.

One day just as the wind started carrying the dried tree pieces along the streets, Taursus took Daemon to the huge salty water. The soldiers were all climbing aboard a floating nest tied in the harbor.

Taursus called him to come aboard the floating nest. To do so Daemon had to cross from the land to the nest over a narrow, flat piece of tree. As he moved cautiously, following Taursus over the water, he lost his footing. He plummeted into the water amid the loud guffaws and yells of the soldiers waiting behind him to cross. Ashamed, he swam to the bank and with his tail between his legs climbed again up to the plank. This time he made it.

The days on the floating nest passed slowly for Daemon. He had plenty to eat and a place in the sun. Of course, no one but Taursus dared to approach him. The real problem was that he was bored. There were no animals or humans to chase. The soldiers spent their time throwing metal pieces at each other and drinking the sour stuff. And Daemon felt the inaction. There was no place to run without bumping into someone or something. Waiting had never appealed to him. He put his paws up on the ship's rail and looked down into the salty water. He was tempted to jump in and get away, but having once been doused and humiliated by that water, he stayed. And finally the floating nest stopped. It was tied down. Still it rocked with the wind and even one or two of the departing soldiers fell off the plank and into the water. Daemon watched the plank shimmying back and forth and jumped instead over the rail. He had seen the soldiers who fell get to shore. He knew he could swim better than they. And soon he was sitting on the bank waiting for Taursus.

On the journey Daemon walked or ran beside Taursus. They traveled behind a few horsemen, many foot soldiers and supply carts. Daemon was the only dog. They went over many fields and even through populated places built of stone and wood. Humans they passed gave the cohort of Romans and their huge bright-eyed dog a wide berth.

Daemon grew even stronger from the walking and running. He liked seeing and smelling all the different trees and animals. He was given food to eat and often it was what Taursus himself ate. He was never hungry. He slept at Taursus' feet when they stopped. Often they walked all night and stopped in an oasis or a cave to sleep during the heat of the day. One night shortly before morning, the first bold bird call woke Daemon in the lightening darkness. The soldiers were up and on their way to the largest city of the conquered people when they met some fishermen coming up a dirt road, each with a string of fish. The fishermen stood back as the soldiers passed, but Taursus stopped beside them with Daemon.

"Give me that big flat fish," he ordered the nearest fisherman.

"That fish is for my wife," the man replied, "but I would be happy to give you any of the others."

All that Taursus did was to point at the man. All he said was "KILL."

And as Daemon tore into the man, his string of heavy fish plopped onto the ground. His screams pierced the still-starlit heavens. A fountain of blood gurgled forth. The other fishermen dropped their lines of fish and ran back up the trail from whence they had come.

Daemon raised his bloody muzzle at the death of the man. Shivering with the thrill of conquest he waited a signal from Taursus to pursue the fleeing companions. After one unprovoked killing he always hankered for more. Instead he felt a cold heavy fish hit his chest. He whirled angrily.

"Eat up, dog." Taursus laughed. "You got us more than we asked."

Daemon struggled to quiet the rush of energy pulsating within his chest. He reined himself from charging Taursus. Instead he wound another layer of hatred upon the hard ball within his stomach. He lowered his head. Driven by frustration, he began licking his blood-covered paws. Not until he smelled the odor of flint and saw the soldiers gathering twigs did he settle to eat. They started a camp fire. They pierced the many kinds and sizes of fish with sticks and began singing and roasting their breakfast.

Daemon lay with the fish between his paws. He began stripping it of its scales and he put his bloodied nose into its insides. In there he found luscious eggs, soft and ripe. He slurped those up first. Then he bit into the flesh, crushing and snapping the bones.

When the morning light lit the camp and the trees were in silhouette, Taursus took him to the lake from which the fish had been caught. He walked with him into the water and washed him. He dipped his helmet and dumped it over Daemon. Then he slapped him on the rump and walked briskly back up the slope to where embers still glowed and the smell of cooking fish still hung in the morning haze.

Taursus offered Daemon some cooked millet. The soldiers had eaten their fill and wanted no more. They had found olive trees ripe with dark small fruits and in the oasis, melons such as they had never eaten in their native land. They gorged themselves until satisfied; then they removed any heavy armor and stretched out under the trees of the oasis. They covered their eyes with handkerchiefs to block out the light. They would sleep there until late afternoon.

Usually Daemon would begin his rest at Taursus' feet. He kept alert for any movement of the cohort. But while they slept he would wander in large circles over the sandy fields. It was allowed. If he met shepherds with their sheep, he would be tempted to kill. But the most that he did was to chase the small lambs until they fell exhausted. The ewes and rams would charge at Daemon to drive him off, but he never fretted that. In fact, he loved the game of it. He had been chased by lions and leopards, bulls and bears in the amphitheater and none had caught him. These animals here in the field were used to wolves, hyenas and coyotes, an occasional mountain lion. Never, he sensed, had they encountered a death machine such as Daemon. He would leave when he decided, not when they chased him off. He had great memories of the two times he had driven a lamb to such exhaustion that it had died in fright. When he had had enough, he would lope back to the men and dream for a while at Taursus' feet.

Daemon was not allowed into the big city when they arrived. The place was surrounded by large blocks of stone piled on top of each other so high that no one, not even a spry mountain goat could surmount the wall. Around its perimeter were smells of animal urine and dung which spoke to Daemon of what arrived today, yesterday and before. Inside the metal gate humans blew horns as they did in the amphitheater when the hunter went in. The soldiers laughed and jostled each other when they saw the bright red ribbons and tightly-clad young women smiling enticingly.

Taursus argued with a gatekeeper as the others filed past him. Daemon sensed Taursus' anger and opened his mouth in a slit, bared his teeth and snarled. He watched a guard come from inside the crowd, shifting his hand to the hilt of his sword. He saw his other hand pointing down at him and his head in a vigorous shake. He also sensed fear. So he stood stiffly on all four paws, his lip raised above his sharp big teeth. He waited for his order to kill. But it did not come. Instead a Roman leader of soldiers, a Centurion, came from behind the large stone wall to join the three men at the gate. He said something to Taursus while he too kept his hand on his short broad sword. He pointed up on the tall wall behind him to two soldier guards watching the exchange. Daemon could tell that Taursus was not pleased. Taursus threw down his hands. He turned from the gate and with one swift, strong motion of his heavily muscled arms he lifted a large stone from the road and threw it at an urn which smelled of fresh water. The urn shattered and the water ran in trickles. Daemon lapped it up.

"Wait here," Taursus ordered Daemon, "and stay." "Stay" meant that Daemon could not chase the animals now going through the gate: sheep and lambs, goats, turtle doves. Why could all those enter and not Daemon?

CHAPTER III

Encounter

Almost the whole night an unhappy Daemon waited behind a broken cart among the weeds far from the vast gate. He lay flat on his stomach, his legs extended behind and in front and his huge head nestled on his front paws. As the first rays of dawn rose and lit the gate, three scraggly curs approached him, but shifted their long, mangy legs and backed away when he stared them boldly in the eyes. He didn't even have to rise up. It was almost as if he hypnotized them. But then came a larger, brown, wolfish-looking dog, spotted with sores, which walked stiffly, his hair bristling above him. Daemon watched as the other curs backed away at his approach. Showing his eagerness to fight, Daemon jumped to all fours and waved his tail low to the ground. He made no sound, but his lips curled upward revealing his large teeth and partly black gums.

Unexpectedly, the brown, street-wise dog turned and trotted away, but with a sidewise glance at Daemon and a flick of his tail, held taut over his back, as if to say, "not now, but later." That challenge was too much to resist. Daemon looked to all sides for Taursus. He knew the penalty for leaving his post, but he would make quick work of the wolfish-looking one and get back to the gate before Taursus returned.

Except that in the short time it had taken him to decide for disobedience, the free, mangy dogs had run off so swiftly that they were nowhere to be seen. As he followed their scent around the crowd, he came closer to the big wall. He smelled where the curs had rubbed their backs against its rough-hewn stones. He pushed hard against the same wall, massaging his muscular frame until his back right leg beat a pattern on the ground.

Then satisfied with his exercise, he stopped and moved on. When he came to a corner turn though, he hesitated. What if Taursus came back for him? He wasn't afraid of Taursus. He could fight him, but he could not fight a whole cohort. He didn't worry that they would kill him. He worried more that they would no longer feed him. He turned slowly. He would go back the way he had come.

Then a scream rang out beyond the bend, somewhat faint. A human scream. He couldn't resist. He whirled back toward the sound. Then as he got closer, pounding and more sharp, breathless screams rose from above, ending with a huge plop of something which fell from the wall upon the path ahead. From the joyful mélange of dog sounds he knew they were upon the prey. The human prey.

Next he heard them, with lighter yelps and sighs, retreat before another, demanding snarl. Daemon knew it was the big brown wolfish dog pushing aside the others and sinking his teeth into the human who had fallen or been pushed over the wall. As he listened Daemon could almost feel the warm blood roll over his own teeth and almost glory in the contents inside the human victim, not fully digested, but sour smelling and full of oil.

Forgetting Taursus in the heat of the moment, he sped around the corner and ran into the commotion. The skinny mongrels were weaving their tall legs anxiously on the outskirts, watching their leader as he satisfied his hunger on the still live, but barely so, human. Daemon stood on a small hill surveying all of them. Then he braced his feet and lowered his head. As he flattened his ears tightly against his head he knew instinctively that Taursus would be proud of his fearsome looks. Just as the human on the ground emitted his last gurgling sound, the big brown dog lifted its bloody muzzle. It had felt, not heard Daemon arrive.

Daemon did not move an inch. He stood with his lip lifted to expose his large strong teeth. As he stared at the brown dog his pupils enlarged, and became flecked with sparks of green.

It was apparent to the three dogs waiting in the weeds that Daemon had the advantage. Both challengers showed their running experience by their taut muscles. Both, from the look in their eyes, were wary and had come out of bad situations and fights. But one was almost twice as heavy, had a larger jowl, a thicker neck with a metal collar to protect it. This one had the advantage of being fed daily with rations intended for strong, fighting soldiers of the Roman army, and these rations filled out his ribs and made his coat shine.

The other, although strong in a rangy way and fearsome to those watchers with less endurance, had a rough coat, many scars and was thin in a way that showed his meals were not guaranteed. With most adversaries, he usually won a contest through snarls and bluffing, thus reserving his energy. However, he realized that this adversary

27

would not be cowed that way. He would have to fight. Could this newcomer hold up against four dogs? So the big brown dog looked to his pack followers to make certain that they would help him pull down this huge intruder the way they often helped with a kill, the way they had helped kill tonight when the human fell over the wall. They, however, to a one, turned sideways, averted their gaze from the brown leader and refused to acknowledge his request. It would have to be his own fight unless the big dog showed weakness. If he did, then they would jump in. Otherwise they would slowly disappear into the gathering darkness.

The big brown dog had lived a long time. He too had learned when to fight and when to retreat. He was not afraid of Daemon. But he was hungry. If Daemon defeated him, Daemon would eat the meat he wanted, leaving the remainder that he did not want, to the three waiting followers.

The big brown dog lowered its tail and sat. Then he lowered himself to the ground and so very slowly and cautiously rolled over, exposing his tender stomach in surrender, and watching Daemon as he came slowly towards him.

Seething with contempt Daemon sniffed his stomach and genitals. Daemon urinated; then slowly, strongly and deliberately he scratched the ground with his powerful hind feet. Just before he pounced upon the prone human, Daemon heard a horn blowing. It was a noise he heard often and he knew the soldiers were gathering for a march. Suddenly it came back to him: where he was; what he was doing; the trouble he was probably in. He whirled. Ignoring the prone enemy and the sweet, enticing meat of the downed human, he galloped away as fast as he could to return to his post, hoping Taursus would not get there first.

But he did.

CHAPTER IV

Discovery

When Daemon reached the huge gate, the soldiers were straggling out. As they emerged each looked at Taursus who was shaking his fist and cursing and screaming Daemon's name. Daemon, silent as a shadow, sneaked behind the gathering carts of food in an attempt to reach the broken cart unobserved. But Taursus saw him.

"Okay," he shouted to his comrades. "Draw your swords! Prepare to send this Daemon back to the underworld!" Sword raised he ran toward Daemon, but two others stopped him. One was the leader.

"Wait up," the leader cautioned. "He wasn't so far away. What if the cur had to shit? Shouldn't he go somewhere that we wouldn't step in it?"

By this time most of the cohort had assembled, and they were arguing good-naturedly among themselves whether the dog or the man was at fault. Daemon could feel the anger of some, the good will of others. He simply sat at ready. If Taursus came toward him, if he threatened, Daemon would take him on before the others could stop him.

Daemon and Taursus both felt the crowd shift at the same time. It was as if they were back in the amphitheater and the emperor had signaled with a "thumbs-up" that Daemon should live. So, after that, because he was forced into it by peer pressure, Taursus agreed that probably Daemon was out in the bushes relieving himself. Daemon felt the release from immediate attack, but he also felt the tension building in Taursus. Taursus did not like to lose face. He would surely do something to revenge this.

Taursus' face was drawn and he smelled of fermented grapes. His tunic was torn on one sleeve and his heavy fist had a smear of blood. But the soldiers no longer were listening to him. The leader announced: "We are going to Galilee, up the Jordan and into the hill country, but it is a long way. We will be marching for three days; so first we will eat." He handed each one a dried plant piece such as the Romans used to give orders to each soldier to send him into battle. Daemon remembered watching humans in the country make these pieces. They cut down tall plants with curved tools, then sliced and pressed them flat. When dry, humans could write on them. Taursus took his piece from the soldier who held it out to him. But he would not look at it. He crammed it unread into the slit in his tunic.

Soon one of the soldiers who supervised the daily meals appeared with some well-groomed humans who were pushing a large cart with food. The cart had fruit and little stick-like pieces of young, field-grazing animals that had been roasted.

Each soldier stood in line for a serving of fruit and meat, and filled his water skin with fresh water from another cart. Taursus filled two skins and then, after one bite of his rations, disgustedly dropped all the food on the ground near Daemon. Daemon smelled the sourness of Taursus which told him that Taursus would not eat today. In fact, Taursus had another canteen of the fermented stuff and he was already gulping it. Daemon gorged himself on the food, but misgivings stirred within him as they started down the slope from the gate, past a graveyard and then past a dump of interesting smells and well-worn castoffs.

Later in the day as they approached the summit of a far hill, Daemon smelled decay. It stopped him. He felt an odd sensation which tumbled from his head down through his tail. What was it that grabbed his tail and slumped it down? This was a new sensation. As his nose palpitated and pulled in the smell, he started to drool. He followed the smell to its source. Something against the sky. He saw two branches crossed upon each other and stuck into the ground. Secured to the cut pieces was a form that looked from this distance like a huge torn rag. But as the wind brought the odor from behind the thing, Daemon recognized the ripe smell of a dead dog.

The soldiers saw it too. They began pointing and yelling. "Look," they said. "A crucified dog! Wonder in whose bower he was making it!" Coarse laughter.

Their guide stopped when he could no longer ignore the pointing. "Yes," he said with a touch of anger. "It is a watch dog. Fine watch dog. He hangs there because he failed to give notice, and as a result five good Roman soldiers died in their beds!"

"Did the army get a new watch dog?" Taursus muttered. Daemon understood that Taursus was still angry and suspicious, that he had no love for Daemon. Only for himself. Taursus would feed him and allow him to live as long as he followed orders, but he would be watching more closely for a slip up, as close as his drunken habits permitted. Daemon never wondered about his own future. What would become of him when he grew old? He had seen older animals let into the amphitheater when the Editor had not enough young ones. They were ripped apart for the crowd's pleasure. They were slower and often lacked enough anger to put on a good show. So they were not a popular event.

Daemon did prefer his new life to his old in the amphitheater. In the amphitheater he had more opportunities to scare, slash, dominate and kill, to watch and smell death. But now he was free of that cage which had kept him from stretching and jumping. Now he was never starved.

After a particular deft kill of an enemy's horse Taursus had told him: "Nobody needs to starve you to make you fight. You use your fangs to rip and kill anything I order. You are like Zeus, powerful and strong." Daemon had always believed that he would obey Taursus as long as Taursus stayed strong, but now he wondered if Taursus would want to keep him.

After a long hot journey, late in the day they came into hill country and refreshed themselves in a flooded river. They shuffled carefully in, pushing through vegetation, which grew profusely on the bank, but was now buried from sight by the rising waters. Cold air rushed down on them chilling their skin and cooling the metal bracelets some wore. The air was cooler than the water they bathed in. It was moving swiftly, bending saplings almost to the ground and the sky was darkening like the ceiling of a sheep pen blackened by the shepherd's fire. The soldiers hurried to finish washing though it was still early evening. Taursus spoke petulantly with one who usually went for the sour liquid with him. He was making an offer. But he didn't like the answer. So he slammed down his shield and walked off from them. He yelled at them as they started on, eager to find a place before dark to shelter from the coming storm.

Taursus picked up his canteen of fermented juice and lifting his head to the sky, downed a few gulps. Then he called Daemon over. "Come, dog," he said. He had never given him a name. When Daemon walked slowly over to Taursus, Taursus offered him a drink from the fermented juice. Daemon did not open his mouth, but Taursus took off his sword and inserted it between Daemon's front teeth. Then he poured what was left into his throat.

Daemon choked and coughed and spit up most of the sour liquid. Then Taursus grabbed his spiked collar and undid it. He laid it on the sand and croaked at Daemon: "Now if you can't be a man and handle your liquor, you will lose your protection. Any wild animal that attacks you will be able to split your neck and drain you." Daemon wasn't scared. He felt pleased instead to be released from the collar. He knew that without it the man lost some control. He was sure now he would not allow himself to be beaten. He would kill Taursus if he tried. With all the others in the cohort gone it would be easy. Not quick. Quick was not as fulfilling as slow and methodical. He would produce, out here in a deserted wilderness, a stunning amphitheater feat that would bring the crowd roaring to its feet.

But Taursus had no present plan to harm him. Instead he walked over to the river and cut the ropes that bound some conquered person's fishing nest. "Get in," he barked drunkenly. Daemon was glad to have shed his heavy collar. He moved his shoulders from right to left and stretched his neck to release his tension. He jumped easily into the rocking boat and sat facing Taursus. He saw that Taursus had removed his own coverings and piled them on the bank. What he now showed in his nakedness was a chain on his hairy chest. From it swung a metal piece with some kind of marks. It must be Taursus' collar.

Taursus grabbed the oars, and was amazingly able to power the boat despite his drunken lurching. He rowed out to the middle of the river and then deliberately dropped the oars into the water to let the boat fight its own way down the river. The boat moved swiftly. Lightning lit the sky and a tree crashed from the right bank, its top branches grazing the side of the boat. Taursus sang a drinking song and pounded his chest. The boat spun round and round, dizzying its occupants. And it circled thus faster and faster missing large broken branches, another boat broken in pieces, a gazelle tossed up and down and shrieking in terror. When one large branch hit the side of the boat, it jolted Daemon. But Taursus seemed unimpressed. In fact, when the boat lurched to one side taking on a load of water, he laughed insanely and threw his great weight to that side as well.

It was more than the sturdy little craft could take. It groaned and broke, throwing Taursus into the water. Daemon tried to scratch-hold to the piece of the boat which was tossed up and down in the swift swells, but he slipped loose and floundered in the water. With his large jaws he then grabbed a piece of the seat board which whirled beside him. He held on until another missile, a barrel from someone's night time party on the beach, came plummeting down the raging river towards him. He saw it, but he couldn't duck fast enough. It caught him on the side of his head and he lost his hold on the seat board. He also lost consciousness.

Somehow the water revived him. In between its rushings which drew him down into troughs and then covered him with foaming spray, he sputtered for air. His eyes played tricks. When he was lifted high and got a glimpse of what was around him, he saw charging toward him a dead field animal and a splintered tree. He could not tell if he was seeing one or two of each. Desperately he half floated and half struggled around them to get to the bank. Every part of him ached as his feet touched bottom. With all his strength he pulled against the water, slamming himself down tight when it pulled him back into the melee. Finally, his feet losing their grasp, and regaining it just a few inches at a time, he worked his way out. The bank on which he landed was far from the one from which they had embarked. The one on which Taursus had left his shield, sword, armor and clothes and Daemon's spiked collar.

After a very short pause, because he had not been born a quitter, he re-entered the raging water. Therein, in the traveling tree he met his match and almost drowned. Therein, from that water, he learned fear, a fear that no one or nothing else, not even any beast in the amphitheater, had been able to instill.

Afterwards he wandered in the pounding rain and dark while streaks of light split the sky. He knew now that Taursus was dead. He didn't see his naked body. It probably went crashing down the river with the debris and the terrified gazelle. He didn't smell death as he had in the amphitheater, but he knew in his bones that Taursus was dead. That gave him a thrill and he urinated against the river weeds and defecated there as well.

He had never had an independent life. From puppyhood he had lived under the Romans, quite the same as their conquered peoples. He had been aware that the fighter dogs and the people who served the Romans had the same outlook. The Romans were boss. If you obeyed you had a chance. If not, there was the amphitheater, or a quick dispatch with a sword, and as he lately discovered, a crucifixion. It depended on the will and amount of time of the Roman. But although Daemon had done as he was ordered, he never really surrendered his will; he was always waiting his time. He hated lying at Taursus' feet and waiting for the signal to eat, come or watch. He stayed for the signal to torment and kill. Killing and tormenting were his connection with Taursus. When Taursus grew old or disabled, Daemon would have his way. Now with Taursus dead he wondered: Would the Roman soldiers be looking for Daemon now? Would they want him as theirs?

At the same time, far up the river just halfway from where the lake fed into the river, the soldiers were gathering Taursus' personal belongings from the shore. They would be sent back to his family in Rome where the drunken man would somehow receive a hero's tribute.

"Look," one of the youngest soldiers yelled, "the dog's collar!" He jokingly put it around his own neck and danced in the sand.

"Enough," the leader said curtly. "Put the collar with the rest. Let this be a signal to all of you. If you are going to get plastered, don't get in a boat during a storm. Taursus was an idiot. His body may even now have floated down to Jerusalem. However, he will be honored in Rome and somehow receive a hero's tribute. Certainly he doesn't deserve it. The fishes will have a feast and I will have to write something of praise to send with his belongings. It will be hard. I could better write in praise of the dog. I am truly sorry to have lost such a ferocious one. The only smart thing Taursus ever did was to pull him from the amphitheater. I always felt a bit safer with his watching us when we were on the move . . . even though I also watched my back when he was near. It is truly a sad day to lose him. Of course, we don't know that the dog died. I do know that he wasn't a heavy drinker," he said with a sarcastic grunt. "But if we meet him again, even with all the loose dogs in and around the towns we will know it is Taursus' dog by his looks. With his one short ear he will stand apart from all the others. If we find him, we will know him and we will take him back."

CHAPTER V

Intervention

Daemon was miles from the search crew. It was a hot morning, but unlike the sweltering heat of his home city, there was a breeze blowing. The hills rose up on all sides and there were plenty of springs and water sources. The rocks here were a medium color, contrasting with his own black paws and the brightness of the mountain sheep looking down from a ledge above. In fact, they were the color of the sweet, sticky liquid that the soldiers got from the bees and put on their cereal, and sometimes made a brew of. He liked climbing off-path through the rocky hills. Jumping from one rock to another, he avoided the prickly tall plants with their pointed needle-like leaves. There were trees, but they had small leaves and the needle trees had tufts on top. He was very hungry, almost as hungry as when he had been starved in the amphitheater. He sensed that it would be hard to run a long time in this condition. He would have to spurt and catch something to eat. It had been a long time, in fact, it had been never that he had caught an animal for his meal. He walked on. From the smells that he encountered he knew that he was retracing back on land the distance he had covered in the boat. Except that he was now on the other side of the river.

There were caves in the hillsides and he went into them hoping to find young animals waiting to be fed.

That didn't happen, and when he chased a small animal with ears that stood straight up, he was unsuccessful. He sensed that the animal had been watching him and that when he gave chase, it lured him where it wanted. But he could not stop himself from chasing it. He was starving. Unlike in the amphitheater, when he cornered prey here, he would forgo tormenting it. He would eat.

He wandered up and down the river bank and into the hills. On the river he saw dark birds that stood on one leg and dipped there beaks into the water. They came up with fish that made his mouth water. But when he plunged in after them, all he came up with was a mouth full of water. He was equally unsuccessful in catching any fish.

Finally, when he had almost returned to the place where the soldiers had met the river on their march from the large gated city, he left the riverside and climbed up the hill. He was less cautious now, striking at anything that moved. He was learning that his obedience to Taursus, who never allowed him to catch field animals, was not a good thing. It would have been better had he disobeyed and caught them on his forays away from the camps. Of course, he didn't think far into that, about what his disobedience would have brought him. He did remember swinging from the rope in the amphitheater. That usually stopped him from any open disobedience.

As the sun began its downward spiral Daemon climbed higher into the hills. Suddenly he heard a sound coming from the undergrowth. He knew a distress signal when he heard it. He stopped and tested the incoming breeze, letting the air sift through his slightly-moving nostrils. What he got was "fowl in distress." At the same time he heard a fluttering of wings and looking down the hill towards the noise he could see amidst the weeds and near a young tree, something moving. He sensed other activity as well. Large and determined. But he ignored it. This time he would get what he was after. He needed food. Throwing caution to the wind he pushed through the weeds.

A human suddenly appeared above the tallest weeds, a huge man with a peeled branch in hand who also bent towards the target. Daemon was not concerned. He would have no trouble with this one. He would beat any human in a race. And if the human got there first, he would easily frighten him into dropping the prize and retreating. But as he closed in rapidly, he paused. His senses, scarcely working because of his overwhelming hunger, now went on full alert. His nose tingled. His head ached. This was a new smell. Coming from a third actor. Acrid. Muscular. Large and feline. Echoing the hunts in the amphitheater. Crashing through Daemon's head and tumbling over each other were memories of large cats slashing and screaming and killing so many of the fighter dogs, not that long ago.

When the large spotted cat jumped from a tree branch, stretching its body and neck toward the man, Daemon acted instinctively, not to protect the man. He was back in the amphitheater and he swerved quickly to his left, braced his heavy feet and caught the descending cat's throat from below in a grip which almost cracked his own neck. They rolled on the ground. Daemon knew it was death for one of them. In the amphitheater it would take at least four fighters to go against a cat. Out here he had no help. There was no one but himself. When they connected, their rolling bodies had knocked the branch from the man's hand and it had clattered down the embankment. The man himself had fallen, but had quickly risen. He did not run away from the fiercely-tangled pair, but instead moved closer.

Daemon paid no attention to the man. The cat was using its claws to flay his sides. He felt the skin over his ribs tear, but because of the way they had connected, the cat had not found his soft stomach. The cat slowed down, gasping angrily. Daemon held on and then, suddenly, he felt the cat shudder as it was pounded by something hard. He knew a blow had struck its head. It reverberated through his own head, so connected to the animal's throat, jolting him sideways and almost throwing him off. But he hung on. In fact, he clamped down harder until his teeth slid deeper and punctured a blood vessel. As the cat gasped its last breath and its claws released his sides, Daemon let go his hold on its neck. He rolled away. He wanted to lick himself and attend to his wounds, but he had to remain vigilant. The large man was standing beside the cat. He might have to fight him too. He knew that he was the one who had hit the cat. A round rock lay a few feet down the path.

As he watched, the man stood straight. He folded his hands. He was ignoring Daemon and mumbling up at the sky. His robe – Daemon smelled it was made of the skin of the desert beasts of burden – was stained with blood. Then he came closer to Daemon and Daemon smelled some of his own blood on it as well as the cat's. He pulled back his lip. He didn't growl, however, because he was confused. Never had a human intervened in such a fight. In the amphitheater it would have been a fight to the death – cat or dog. Why had this human intervened? Why had he helped? Unlike most humans he showed no fear, even now when the smell of death pierced the twilight. This man was unafraid like himself. Like Taursus. But he had no large teeth for protection; no smell of fermented fruit hung upon him. Yet his body was relaxed, his spirit settled.

Suddenly Daemon was hungry again. The fluttering in the weeds had stopped but Daemon smelled the small creature's fear. He perked up his ears and looked toward the weeds.

The man followed his gaze and strode two paces into the weeds. He reached down and plucked a brown bird with yellowish streaks from the ground. The bird had only one wing flapping. The other appeared immobile.

The man looked at Daemon and then down at his own robe. Holding on to the bird he kick-swept under the bushes with his sandaled foot. He appeared to be searching for something. Daemon remembered Taursus often lost items of clothing, once even his sword. Daemon knew where they lay but would never retrieve them.

Unable to locate what he was looking for, the man stopped looking. He stood indecisively shifting from one sandaled foot to the other. "I will be back," he said looking at Daemon. He did not say "Stay." "Stay" was the word Taursus used over and over when he left Daemon outside bars and amphitheaters and most recently, the big city of the conquered people. Then the man disappeared on a narrow path to Daemon's left.

CHAPTER VI

Gratitude

Darkness fell swiftly. Daemon smelled the strong cat death smell as he lay licking his side. The blood had stopped oozing and was beginning to congeal. He was hungry, but still weak and could not decide if he would sleep first or continue on his search for food. Sleep won out and he dozed until he sensed movement around him. There was a moon, not bright because of a swath of cloud, but bright enough that he could detect shapes moving in the darkness. The shapes looked like old dogs with slanted backs. Hair stood straight up on those backs. They were heavy through the middle and their legs shorter behind as if dragging. They were striped dark on a lighter coat and had box-like heads and pointed ears. Those heads were similar to dark bear heads but with larger, more pointed ears. They squeaked, squealed and cackled softly to each other, and then he heard them ripping into the carcass of the cat. He sensed that they would also come his way and was not surprised when he felt a hot stinking breath on his back leg. Immediately he pulled a ferocious growl from his stomach up through his throat, swiftly tucked his legs under him and turned a quick circle to face the invader.

Almost as quickly the invader yelped and jumped away. But not far away, and soon there were others circling with her. Kind of the way the fighter dogs circled their own prey, keeping out of range, but testing the victim's abilities with short runs towards him, coming closer and closer and knowing that if the hunted one chased one of them, the others would attack from the rear. Daemon sensed he could not outrun them. There were too many and he was already exhausted from lack of food and loss of blood. But he would fight. He would take some of them with him before they got his body to devour.

They swarmed now upon the cat. The largest female sat atop the beast pulling and tearing its neck. Another routed its stomach and slurped up the contents. Snarling and snapping very close to Daemon, two others vied for a strip of meat ripped from its side. He even heard the sound of a snapping bone which told him that these invaders had strong teeth and jaws.

Daemon felt stirrings in his own wounded sides as the feast continued. Soon they would tire of the cat and come for him. They were in no hurry. They knew he could not escape. They would soon allow their pups to the scene. He had seen it all many times before, especially when Taursus had allowed him to leave the camp and investigate while the soldiers slept. With all the adults sated there would be no reason not to allow the young ones to do their own ripping and eating. And after they all left and the area was clear of invaders, the fowl would come from the sky and pick clean the bones. His bones and the cat's. Finally, as he had seen many times, the crawling insects would get the very tiniest morsels and carry them away.

The clouds had cleared from the moon when the first invader actually attacked Daemon. She grabbed for his rump and Daemon slashed back cutting open her boxy jowl which ran with dark blood and slivers of bone. But then three others approached with eyes glowing like coals. Daemon crouched as he did in the amphitheater, not making any of his legs available to the invaders. But he was certain that sooner or later they would decide on a mass attack and in their blood lust forget that he could kill some of them. Methodically they moved in and out, toward him and away. Occasionally one would slash at him. One left with a mouth full of tail. Daemon grabbed an ear and tore it away from a bold one, but dropped it quickly to be ready for the next attacker. Finally, as if on a signal, three of them came together shoulder to shoulder, and advanced with their slobbering, bloody faces. Then as if on another signal, silently, they turned an invisible corner and moved backward in synch, swishing their bushy tails the way they had come. He wondered why they retreated. And then he heard it too. A noise of something coming through the bushes. Down the hill from above. Was it another cat? Perhaps the mate of the downed one? He knew he had not the energy to fight. Never again would he take on a cat like that by himself. He would need other fighters with him to parry and feint. And even then, and even in a strong mode, it would be risky.

Around the large stone above there came a light through the darkness. The light grew brighter until Daemon saw beneath it a human figure. He was in a light colored tunic such as the soldiers sometimes used even in the amphitheater. But this robe had no gleaming trim. First he saw the man. Then he used his nostrils. They told him that it was the same man that had been on the path with the cat, the one who had gotten out of the way when they fought, the one who had stoned the cat. He smelled the lighted branch but no other. He also smelled something that made the saliva drip from his mouth. Roasted fowl. The fowl the man had taken had been cooked over a fire. From its smell Daemon detected it was the same one that had been caught in the weeds, though its residual fear smell was nearly gone, actually roasted away. The man was carrying it on a small rope.

Certainly the man was in danger again. This time from a very hungry dog. Ordinarily he would have simply identified the man's weak spot, maybe from his posture or his breathing. He would have made him drop the fowl and then chased him off. He would be lucky to leave with his life. But something dissuaded him. Instead, he stood alert on all four feet, his tail sweeping low and slow. He whined because of the competing emotions inside him. He wanted the food, but he also wanted to know why he could find no weak spot in this man. How could he look at the scene of the dead and stripped cat and the strong fierce dog and show no fear? He had known only one other human who showed no fear and that was Taursus. But Taursus was always drinking that sour juice and Daemon knew that made him bold. In fact, when Taursus had come to the amphitheater for him, then too he had smelled of that juice. Not as much as he did when they took out the boat, but Taursus seemed always to have that juice in him to give him courage.

Daemon was confused by this man's appearance as well. Earlier he had worn an animal skin robe, and his smell and the animal smell blended, as did the smells of a herd of field animals. He no longer wore it. He had very long hair both on his head and his face. His arms were covered with hair that glinted the color of the evening sun. They were strong and muscular as were his legs and Daemon knew that here was a human who might be his equal in a fight, certainly one to be wary of. He watched as the man stuck the pole with the torch into the ground. Together with the light from the moon it made the scene almost as bright as day. Then the man untied the fowl from the rope and tossed it to Daemon.

"Eat up," he said in a smooth deep voice. "I brought it to thank you for saving my life. God knows I would have died under that cat had you not come. I know you were sent by my God. However, I do not know what to do with you. If I leave you, those heathen hyenas will return and devour you. Yet I do not want to be close to you nor touch you. That I cannot do. I cannot take you into my cave; so I will sit here through the night and guard you until you regain your strength."

Daemon watched as the man gathered firewood and surrounded them both with small piles of it. Then he lit those piles, much the way the soldiers had, to take the chill off the night and keep away marauding beasts. Both of them could hear the cackling and occasional snarl in the bushes and knew that the vandals were still watching. Daemon stood up intending to chase them and punish them, but the man put up his hand. He stretched it wide and said "Stay."

Daemon automatically stopped at that word. He knew that one. He looked at the man. He did not want to obey. He had believed he would never obey again and yet he did not want to leave the fowl, the only food he had had in two days.

"Lie down and eat," the man gestured to the fowl. "It's all yours. I had some millet, some grasshoppers and honey. That may not sound good to you, but I fried those little ones in olive oil and they were tasty. I slit the bird's throat, bled it, washed it and cooked it although I doubt you would complain about blood in your food." He laughed a hearty laugh. "I also washed my robe. Your blood, the cat's blood. Quite a mess."

Daemon sensed in his voice an integrity he had never met before. Certainly not from the army men. Certainly not from those who ran the amphitheater. Certainly not from the victims he had been ordered to kill. Certainly not from himself. From somewhere he pulled forth a memory of himself as a really young pup, hunkering down and nursing on a large black female. There were five little ones, himself included. There were only three working teats to give them nourishment. If all three were occupied, he would bite and push one of the other pups away. Then one day a man appeared with a large water-filled urn. The two smallest pups were put into it and held down until they stopped squirming. As young as he was, he had paused but a second before he began pulling even more smugly and roughly on the teat he held. He had no concern for the drowned pups. He had not wanted to share food with them. He was glad they were out of his way.

The way he saw this man . . . he owed Daemon nothing. He didn't have to return with the fire and the food. The vandals would have snuffed out Daemon's life. And he would have been out of this man's way. But this man was not like that. He did what he did because of a need within himself. It had nothing to do with others. Fulfilling this inner demand brought him the unusual balance that puzzled Daemon, an integrity that made it impossible to show a weak spot. Whatever it was in this man that made him different, he returned because of it. Not because of Daemon.

Daemon realized that he was still standing stiff-legged but the man had totally relaxed and had sat down on one of the large boulders. He was picking stones from the ground and lobbing them down the hill.

Daemon could no longer hold off. Looking cautiously at the man to make sure he would not be netted as in the amphitheater, nor have the fowl taken away, he grabbed the fowl, sped to the outermost area of the circle which the fire still lit and began eating. It took him but a few minutes until the bones of the fowl lay undone like the bones of the cat. Still, he licked the bones and separated the little remaining pieces from the bones, allowing their oily lusciousness to finally make their way to his stomach. He was quenched.

Then with a full stomach caution returned. He spun, stiffened and growled and looked directly at the man. Would he come after him with rope or stone? But the man had spread the animal skin he was carrying onto the ground. And he lay upon it. His breathing was coming in very even, strong spurts. Obviously he was here for the night, or at least for a while. Now Daemon remembered how he had slept at Taursus' feet. He had never liked that. Humility and obedience were not his way. He would not lie beneath this man, but as much as he wanted to leave and to catch vandals who were still moving in the bushes, his training told him to stay and protect the campsite. This was his habit. It was a smart thing to do.

The times he had circled the soldiers' camp during the night, the camp was either on level ground or on a hill. From either point he could watch and guard even while he was exploring the near country. But in this spot underbrush grew thick and high enough for men to hide behind. So he lay down inside the circle of light but as far from the man as he could. He did not lie on his side which still ached from the mauling by the cat. Instead he lay on his stomach, back feet and tail tucked close to his body, his large head resting chin-first on the ground between his strong front legs and feet. All the night he jerked and whined in his dreams.

CHAPTER VII

Game Changer

The fires had dimmed to embers when the light came up in the east. Daemon had fallen into sound sleep at the first crack of dawn because he knew that the vandals retreated then to their crevices in the rocks to sleep during the heat of day. Without moving a muscle, ready to strike, he watched the large man rise, kick out the fires, scatter the embers and cover them with dirt which he dug up with the end of a small branch.

Something incongruous about that. Such a large man. Such a small branch. Obviously this man was one of the conquered people the Romans had come to watch. On their trek here Daemon had seen many. The night he had spent at the doors of the city he had seen hordes. Those who smelled similar to this man leaned on large naked branches stripped of leaves. This man's slender branch still wore its skin. Had he lost a large branch?

Now that Daemon was restored with food and rest he wanted to bait this man who continued his clean-up chores. He wanted to fight him − to take him down. What confused him was the signal the man was sending. He sensed this man's gratitude. A mistaken gratitude. He had not fought the cat to protect the man. He had fought the cat for the fowl. As he grew older he had learned to interpret intentions of these humans. He smelled them, heard them, watched their countenances, the gestures of their limbs, the tone of their voices which bespoke their intentions. Always there was a certain posturing, a certain deception. But none appeared in this one. This one had all his parts working together. His voice was not silky and deceptive while his arms moved to catch or harm. It was direct, a clear summer bird call with no hidden meaning. His limbs were not taut, ready to fight. His whole body stood straight and the messages which came from his outside and his inside were identical. He had no bad intentions toward Daemon, in fact, no intentions at all. He did not want to control him. He did not want to capture him and trade him to another for those silver pieces humans used for such business. Daemon tried to raise his lip in a snarl, but it came out more like a whine. He surprised himself.

He heard the man laugh, watched him turn his back and start up the hill. He could attack, pull him down from the back, but something stopped him. Curiosity. Why was this man so different? Surely he had a weak spot. Why had Daemon missed it? He would follow him and see where he went, what he did, how he lived. In time he would discover his fear. Then there could be an attack, an attack on someone who had only done him good. But he hoped that attack would come, like the vandals' attack, in the evening, after the sun descended and all the earth was grey. He would watch and see first. He would satisfy his curiosity. He would not attack until he saw terror in this man's eyes. That was what he always did. The hair on his back would rise and he would stiffen so that he would appear much larger than he was. He hoped this man would fight because the fight could be one of the best, not like the fisherman who only screamed in terror. He

56

wanted a real combat. The cat had left him wounds. He had never bled as much, even in the amphitheater. (He would bleed again someday soon and this time truly because of this man.)

He followed the man up the hill, stiffly at first, his sides aching. But as the sun warmed him, his body loosened. His strong legs carried him faster, so fast that he had to slow down so as not to overtake the man.

As he turned a corner he came upon a cave. In front of the cave was a clearing. He smelled many humans. Many different humans who had been here at different times. These were not Romans. These smells came from the conquered people of this land. Unless the rain had washed their scents away, the Romans had never ever been here. Outside this cave on a large stone lay that camel's hair piece the large man had worn during the cat attack. It lay releasing its moisture in the sun. Beside it was a strip of skin that had holes in it and a polish on it. Daemon knew the name for this skin. Taursus used to yell: "Where is my belt?" Because he had heard the word so often Daemon knew what it meant. In fact, he always knew where Taursus' belt lay. He smelled where it was. He could have brought it to Taursus, but one of the few ways that Daemon could disobey without repercussion was to pretend ignorance. He was just a dumb dog, good only for fighting and killing. But he was a dumb dog that enjoyed tricking his master. Taursus never knew about his cunning ways. Daemon reveled in his disobedience. He was always waiting for Taursus to show fear, and then he would attack. But now that could never be. He would never have dominance over Taursus. They had been separated forever.

Daemon walked over to the camel skin.

"Back," the large man came walking swiftly from the cave with his hand extended and held up in front of Daemon.

Daemon automatically backed up. He knew the word as a command. Just as he knew "sit," "lie," "stay," "come," "eat," and "kill."

The man picked up the camel skin. He tossed off the light-colored covering he was wearing which came slightly below his knees. He wiggled into the camel robe. Keeping his eyes on Daemon he backed into the cave and came out immediately with a small skin container that he attached to his head with a strip of dead field animal. Daemon could smell the skin of the little animal on it, such a one as he had chased in the fields. He sat with his nostrils working toward the large man and knew that inside the dead-skin box were pieces of the same thin, dried-plant pieces on which the Romans wrote orders.

When he finished dressing, the large man came over to Daemon. He stood a good distance from him rubbing his head. "I don't know what to do about you," he mused. "I heard today that a Roman soldier and his dog died in the river. I could give you back to them just in case you are that dog. I don't want to do that, but if they start accusing the people I serve of stealing or killing the soldier and his dog, I might have to. At the very least I would tell them where they can find you." He rubbed his head again. "But you know," he said, "If I speak about you and tell them of you, they might decide that either I or my people know something we don't know, and they might kill us, even crucify us. They seem to enjoy that. Perhaps it is best to say nothing at all and to let you take off into the hills where we found each other."

With that, he walked back over to the cave entrance. He turned around in front of the cave. Looking at Daemon he opened and extended both hands and said in a strong deep voice "Out." He said it first in the conquered people's language, then in the one Daemon heard from Taursus. Without that spoken command Daemon would have understood what he meant from his hand signal. He put "out" in his memory bank of words. What he couldn't decide is if he would obey.

Later that day the large strong man started down the hill. He walked without a branch to lean on. He never looked back. Daemon watched until he disappeared and then listened to his footsteps as they became more and more faint. He sat looking at the cave. He arose and walked slowly to the entrance. He looked inside. Toward the front left side there was a place where fires were made and the ceiling of the cave was black with the soot from those fires. Obviously the man had built a fire last night. The smell lingered despite efforts at clean up. Daemon could still identify grease beneath the slight covering of sand which had been thrown over the pit. That grease still smelled of the fowl he had been given. He knew that this was where the man had cooked it. There was a jug of oil, a large pot and a neat pile of sticks and straw. He had seen the Romans build fires this way and he looked and smelled for the flint piece like the one they used. He found it first with his nose, on a shelf-like piece of rock near the pile of sticks.

On the other side of the cave, far in back and faintly visible, was a pad of various animal skins. Even from the cave entrance Daemon could smell a mix of large field animals and the man who had slept on them, wafting toward him. Beside the pad was a rolled-up, leather-covered packet filled with the type of dried plant sheets which Daemon recognized as the same material that the man sometimes wore in a leather capsule on his head. Except that this leather packet was much, much larger, and older. It smelled of age and also of the man's own skin oil. Farther back in the cave he could hear water burbling which told him that a spring visited this cave.

He needed to see more. He remembered the new command, "out." But he would not obey. Instead he would enter the cave. He would roll on his back, legs in the air, on the pad of animal skins. He would drink from the burbling spring. He would steal anything that he could from this large man and then leave. He became more and more excited as he remembered similar episodes in the past. In his mind's eye he saw the leg of lamb that he snatched from the partying wagon drivers who accompanied the Roman army contingent. Taursus had found him with it, but he only laughed when he heard the drivers yelling. They had roared into Taursus' camp brandishing sticks, looking for Daemon. They saw him near Taursus' tent, dragging the leg, his lip rolled into a snarl, his tail low and slowly sweeping the ground. But Taursus stood between them and Daemon and only laughed. He said: "Surely this lamb had more than one leg. Go eat the others." He said this with his hand on the hilt of his sword, and like Daemon he stood stiff and tall and seemed to grow bigger as they challenged him. So they went away. Taursus had had plenty to drink that night, Daemon remembered. He didn't stop drinking until he threw down his empty cup in frustration. Then he barely made it into his sleeping sack.

There were other times Daemon had stolen. He never stole from Taursus, not that he liked Taursus, but he had in him a partner in crime and he would not ruin that. In fact, somehow, though he could never put it into words, somehow he knew that it was more enjoyable to steal or kill, to plunder or destroy in the company of another who egged you on, than to do it privately when no one else knew. It was even more pleasurable to steal from those who accompanied the army than to chase the little field animals until they expired and their shepherds shook their fists at you in powerless exasperation. In a way that was what had been so good about the amphitheater. Shared brutal deeds. There a whole amphitheater of watchers yelled you on. Memories of his last bout with the bear flew into his head. He could feel his teeth clamp down on that slobbery throat while the crowd shouted itself hoarse when he refused to obey the Editor. In all that large amphitheater he felt the most powerful.

Right now. If the strong man had not told him "Out," he might have returned into the woods on his own. But it was as if he had to do the opposite of what he was told, just because it was the opposite. He would not take orders from another. He had hated that ever since the day in the amphitheater when Taursus had hung him and swirled him until he obeyed.

He raised one paw, but before he advanced, he heard them. Footsteps coming from below. It sounded like two. They were speaking ardently. They were speaking to each other without any apparent caution, as if they trusted one another. This was unusual. Not the way his Romans spoke to each other with one hand on a sword, even sometimes when speaking with those who slept in the same barracks.

61

Daemon dropped his paw to the ground and retreated slowly, shifting his weight from front legs to back legs. He moved from the face of the cave. He would investigate it later. But for now he did not want to be caught in the cave. He could take on one human, maybe both, but he chose to be cautious. He slinked into the bushes and lay down. "Should he protect the large man's cave?" The idea hit him like a bolt of lightning. It caused him to rise on his haunches. It really confused him. Why should he? He had protected the Romans because he knew they would hurt him, net him and kill him slowly, even crucify him if he didn't. He had no reason at all to protect this one. The large man probably could not hurt him. He was wary of nets, but the large man had no net that he saw or smelled. In fact, and this was truly strange, the large man had no weapons. Daemon lay back down quietly and waited to see who owned the footsteps coming up the hill.

The owners of the footsteps were two young men. They called out at the cave entrance "John!" Not getting an answer they advanced into the cave. Daemon could hear them speaking animatedly. One of them seemed to be trying to convince the other to take some action. Daemon was used to these tactics. Taursus and another had often used them to persuade a third soldier to go for adventure—like the time they had come upon a woman working in her garden with her small child, and had rushed into her nest behind her before she could close the door. They ignored her small child whom she sent scurrying under a table, but they raided her pantry, throwing food they didn't want out in the yard for Daemon. When she softly objected, Taursus struck her to the floor with the back of his hand. As she fell she jarred a table, sending three, warm, fragrant loaves of baked grain-mix tumbling to the floor.

They closed the door before Daemon could run back in and get the loaves. He had gobbled all the spoils thrown him outside, and so he whined and scratched the door to let them know he wanted entry. They ignored him.

Soon Daemon heard thuds, the woman's screams and the soldier's laughter coming from inside. Their terrorizing lasted a long time, and when they finally came out, he could spy no food left on the floor. Each of the soldiers clutched one of those fragrant loaves as he jumped on a horse he had borrowed. They had left the woman lying on the floor, alive, but shaking and sobbing, her small child cowering beneath a table. Daemon lifted one paw, going forward to check for crumbs and to finish the job on the woman and her child. But Taursus called him away.

Daemon had been disappointed that time, even angry. He had sulked. He wouldn't look at Taursus. Not that Taursus noticed. Daemon had expected to be called in for a killing. Instead he was told to follow the soldiers to their open-air sleeping spot. They had had their sport with the woman, and he had been denied his. Taursus knew that Daemon preferred these female humans even to the little field animals; killing them was his signature sport. The fear in their eyes would explode as he plunged his teeth into their smooth, warm skin. They had no courage at all, and they disgusted him. Now, with Taursus dead, Daemon would have no one to stop him from attacking any prey he chose. And he could decide himself if a woman would live or die. He might even spare one, if like the brown cur, she would roll over on her back in submission.

Daemon refocused on the John man. Why should he protect someone's belongings who could not punish him? Why spare someone he could surely kill?

The truth was he already had spared John when he could have taken him down. Didn't that show he was acting more like John than like Taursus? Taursus would not have spared John. And certainly he would not have allowed John to turn his back, to walk away as he did from Daemon. He would have slaughtered him for his disrespect.

In fact, since Taursus' death Daemon's only slaughtering had been in self-defense or to sate his hunger.

Instinctively he knew that, unlike Taursus, John would never urge him on to torment and kill. John would not glory with him in terror. If John found a bird in a trap he would only use as much force as necessary to kill it. John did not even wear armor or a sword or carry a whip. John obviously lived a different way. Yet he was strong and unafraid as a mountain animal which surmounted the highest hill and shook its long horns in the wind.

So why stay here? Was it worth a wait to fight John? He could return to the soldiers with whom he shared the thrill of killing and tormenting. He could find the soldiers' old camp and trail them from there to their new one. But he sensed that if he went back to the army, he would have to obey. They could even send him back to the amphitheater. Here, in contrast, he was free to do as he pleased. He did not want to ever obey anyone again. He would stay for now, trailing these two men and watching what they did. Like a vandal at dusk he hid in the shadows and trotted quietly behind them as they strode away from the cave.

They strode down through the woods, talking earnestly to one another. The one ahead in line stumbled on a branch that had broken in the storm and went down on his knees. The other one did not laugh and berate him. Rather, he stopped and offered his hand which the fallen one accepted. Then the other one waited while the fallen one brushed off his clothing. Daemon flashed back to his own fall off the plank and into the big water. The loud guffaws. The crude jokes. His own shame. This offering here of warmth and help from one human to another was something new.

The sun was bright and hot as they came out of the shaded area onto the beach. Daemon smelled farm animals and plants, people and water, fish that had been dead for a short while lying in boats, and his large man whom the others called "John." He was standing in the water shouting. He waved to the people on boats which were crossing to a landing on the side where the sun went down. John called a warning to them to "straighten up." Maybe Daemon didn't understand the words. But he did understand that order. Many times he had heard the head soldier yell at Taursus to "straighten up." But the head soldier had not done to Taursus what John did to the others waiting patiently on the beach. One by one they would advance, remove their robes and meet John where he was standing hip deep in water. When they got close to him, they would hand their robes to another man standing in the water behind John. They would stoop over and John would push them slowly under the water and on their rising back out, he would pour a ceramic pot of water over each one, looking thoughtful and saying words which sounded important. Then each person would return to the beach and revest. Mostly the crowd on the beach were the conquered people, although mixed in were a few foreign watchers. A Roman or two rounded out the group which held a few Ethiopians, Parthians, Egyptians and Cyrenians. Daemon was familiar with most of these people smells because as gladiators, hunters and planned victims they had been held against their will in the amphitheater.

Daemon slinked from one large bush to another so as to watch the scene without being observed. He rubbed his large head on a small tree which shaded him and licked the gouges in his sides. They still hurt, but itched too and Daemon knew that meant healing. As he lay there he saw the two men he had followed from the cave advance to the water. But the one who had fallen down, backed off and did not follow the other, nor did he allow John to douse him with the water.

The heat from the sun was scorching, even under this small tree. And Daemon was thirsty now and hungry as well. Nonetheless he waited, watching the young men. The one sitting on the beach shook his head dry the way Daemon did after a swim so that the water drops flew in circles around his body and splashed his partner and made him laugh.

As day turned toward evening, the crowd on the beach thinned out. Fewer boats were crossing to the dock on the other side. People who sold food folded up their wares and put them on carts. On the far side a weak person lifted some of his foodstuff from a table, stumbled and spilled most of it onto the ground. He was far from the other vendors who had already left the area. Daemon made a swift decision, raced from the bush to the site of the spill and began eating the meat and fish in their leaf wrappings.

The two young men raced over to Daemon, yelling and waving at him to go. Another came with a huge branch and reared back to throw it at Daemon. Daemon swerved as if to retreat, just long enough that the man was thrown off balance trying to shift the branch to his new position. The pause was just long enough to provide an opening to attack.

"Back," the command rang on the evening air. Daemon growled unhappily. But because of enforced, repetitious training, he moved backwards as he was told. Again he was confused. Again he saw the large man, John, telling him what to do. Should he rush him? Take him down?

Obviously the large man was not concerned or worried about an attack. No fear. As usual he appeared at ease. He walked over to the overturned cart giving his back carelessly to Daemon. He took the tray from the weak man who was shaking and pale. He turned the tray over deliberately spilling its remains onto the ground. Then he signaled the young men to stop waving their branches and come to him.

He took a pouch from the shorter one. Holding it under his arm, he took the weak man's thin hand and pushed open his fingers so that it looked like a "back" signal aimed at the sky. Next John opened the pouch above the weak man's hand and shook it empty. He waved his two young pack members closer. As he handed the empty pouch back to the one from whom he had taken it, he said: "Leave the food on the ground for the dog. Let him have it. He once saved my life."

Daemon did not understand what John was saying, but he felt the bodies before him slowly relax. The cart owner was dancing on the sand the way the soldiers did after battle, though nothing violent had happened here. There were no battle spoils. No one was hurt. All seemed even more glad than after a victorious battle.

John waited until the weak man had run away with his cart and until all the others had left; then he signaled Daemon back to the spilled food. John smiled and walked slowly away and up into the hills.

CHAPTER VIII

Lost Branch

Following at dusk was easy. From the path John had taken, Daemon knew he was returning to his nest. But Daemon did not want to go straight to the cave. He wanted to retaliate against the vandals who went after him last night when he was at his weakest. So he veered off at a different angle toward the temporary campsite John had fashioned. When he smelled the lingering smell of ashes and sun-baked bones, he knew he was near the site. He identified no fresh spoor from the vandals. But immediately to his right, he smelled something which carried the large man's smell. He moved gingerly forward. Was there an animal trap covered with branches? Daemon stopped to listen. "Who, who-o-o-o" came wafting at him, and then a flutter of wings, a squeak as a small animal lost its life to the night bird. Nothing else. Except far off some faint squeals of vandals waking to the night. He wanted to hunt them down and rip them apart, but was reluctant to leave the new smell.

So he stood still among the weeds, smelling the big man's smell and listening to the fading squeals of the vandals. After a long wait, as long as when he was stalking one of the birds which walked on tall sticks, he made his decision and moved cautiously toward the smell. It grew stronger as he approached. But the smell had not been renewed for some hours. It still carried the large man's skin particles, but the dew and all day breezes had softened the smells, telling him the large man was not close. Puzzled he put his nose out and touched the object. It was a sturdy branch, stripped of its bark and with a knob on one end. Gingerly he lifted it in his massive jaws and swung it around. When it hit a sapling, it jarred his teeth and he shook it angrily. Then he swung it again and this time he heard the sapling crack and in the deepening dusk, he saw a small grey stick-form fall off to the side of a dead tree. Was this the large man's weapon? It was heavier than the flat and pointed wooden sticks the hunters practiced with. But it had no sharp point like the soldiers' lances. Then he remembered seeing many branches like this carried by the conquered people who walked along the dirt roads and jumped or fell to the side as the Romans sped up and passed them. After one dousing with mud he learned that if he was running next to the horses when they passed, he would quickly move to the back. He knew that the soldiers would seek the puddles from the morning rain and guide the horses into them in order to splash the people walking with their bundles. He knew it was their fun game.

Now he wondered: "Was the large man missing this branch?" He might have lost it the way Taursus lost his belt. It smelled of many places, including the river into which the large man pushed people when he doused them with water. And they let him.

He could take the branch to the large man. But should he? What would he get in return? He stood hesitant. Then he dropped the branch and trotted up the hill to see what the large man was doing. He owed this human nothing. All that he had done was to give him food twice. He could have gotten that food by attacking the large man. And it would have been more fun than waiting. Perhaps more dangerous, but certainly more fun. Yet he didn't feel quite content with his decision. Something was missing. This man was straightforward and direct. What he said matched his body language and his smell. He was fearless. No one he had ever tricked or attacked was like him. So doubt lingered about abandoning the branch, a doubt which he did not understand. Daemon knew nothing of commitment, of loyalty, of friendship. From puppyhood on he had been raised as a dirty fighter. So now, when something for the first time was stirring inside him and pulling him irresistibly toward a human, he balked.

One thing was clear: he was not welcome inside the large man's cave. When he arrived there a little later, the large man had started a fire and was shaking a cooking vessel with oil. Daemon could smell the oil heating with the little grey spice that looked like the needles on the large trees. And he smelled the grasshoppers as well. The food sizzled and popped. Next to the fire was a plate and on the plate some field animal parts. There was fruit in a basket. John was in his woven covering with his sleeves rolled up. He had removed his head decoration and put it to the side with his camel's hair robe.

When John saw Daemon, he stood straight. Again he extended the fingers of both hands and said the word: "Out!"

Daemon stood stiffly with his lip rolled back against his teeth. But he didn't move forward.

71

It was as if John did not see his anger, his long teeth gleaming in the fire light. John came within two feet of Daemon whose hackles had risen and whose tail had descended.

"Fine," John said. "You are hungry, I see. I thought you would be gone by now. I don't have a problem with feeding you. My people are so generous. Though they have scant to eat themselves, they bring me food from their flocks and gardens. But you must stay outside the cave, and you must not hurt anyone who comes to visit." With that he went back into the cave from which he brought a large piece of field animal, luscious and fresh, over to a spot slightly to the side of the cave. Daemon just watched, and soon John brought one of the skins from his pad and put it beside the meat. There was an overhang above the spot and Daemon knew immediately what the skin was for. Taursus, when he remembered, had put down a skin in a sleeping place. Would John lie down on that skin with Daemon at his feet as Taursus did? Daemon prepared for the contest. He would not lie at this large man's feet. He bristled and emitted a half-hearted growl. John ignored him and walked back into the cave.

Daemon did not follow him in. He lay beyond the entrance watching the large man eat, clean up and then sit with the packet of dried paste sheets in his lap, turning the pieces and looking at each. When the fire became embers, John returned the leather packet to the shelf and lay down. Soon his breath was regular and smooth. Daemon walked back to the animal skin. He picked up the lamb piece next to it, and shook off the tiny insects which swarmed over it and had already taken pieces from it. After he had eaten he tossed the bone down the hill as he had seen Taursus do and he lay down on the animal skin scrunching himself into a ball with his tail curved around his rump and his huge head directed out toward the woods. He slept lightly until morning, and then slowly he felt his caution lessen, not entirely disappear, but lessen. He felt that any danger would not come from John. How could he have predicted his own near-death just a short time later?

The next day and each day thereafter Daemon would roam the hills searching for the vandals and returning at night to John's cave. The vandals were more clever than he could have imagined. Never could he surprise them in their crevices or caves, and sleepy as they were, they would lure him away from those dens. The next time he revisited the dens, nothing remained but the smell. Every morning before he left he would wander close to John's cave, tempted to explore it, but the vandal search and his own confused intentions toward John pulled him away. Every night Daemon would be more and more exhausted from his chases because the vandals kept moving and making their nests farther and farther away. Each night John would return from his river spot and leave something outside the cave for Daemon to eat. One night John stopped beside Daemon's pad. Daemon had just returned from his roaming and was pulling a sticker from the underside of his paw.

John dropped a fair-sized fish next to the pad. He was smiling at Daemon. "You know," he said, "since you have come here I have no more trouble with wild animals. I have lost my good staff, but I have this other one from a friend. I used to threaten the wild animals that came to the cave. Once I had to fight a small leopard and afterwards I had to clean the cave of its blood. It's too bad that you too are unclean. Otherwise it would be good to have you guarding from inside my cave." Daemon did not understand what John was saying, but the large man was relaxed when he said it. Definitely non-threatening. Daemon felt an urge toward being in a pack with John. But how could he be in a pack with someone who didn't want him?

Occasionally toward evening when Daemon returned, he would see that John had visitors in his cave. Two of these were his most frequent visitors. When they came Daemon would go to the outer circle of the firelight and watch them sit and talk animatedly with John. Invariably the shortest one would gesture toward Daemon; point to him where he lay watching them. Then the other two would follow his gaze until they too were looking at Daemon. This man was trying to persuade John to do something. Daemon knew that from having lived with the soldiers and having understood how they decided on raids on towns or families or drunken feasts. This man would invariably point in Daemon's direction. There was no doubt that his intentions toward Daemon were not good and Daemon would growl imperceptively thinking that he might chase Daemon or have someone take him away or kill him.

Daemon was ready to attack the little man if he got the signal. For just this once he would obey John. But John seemed not to take this man seriously. He patted him on the back, and as the two said their good-byes, John gave him a hug as inclusive as the bear hug in the amphitheater. Daemon had not seen men disagree so strongly, yet hug each other nevertheless. This action confused him even more. It was obvious that inside himself this one held no anger nor resentment toward John.

Still struggling with what he had witnessed, Daemon trotted to his bed at the side of the cave and fell into a sleep packed with dreams which twitched his legs and routed yelps and growls from his insides.

Soon after, Daemon stopped worrying about any threat from this short one and dropped his guard toward John's usual visitors, but not entirely.

CHAPTER IX

Submission

One chilly, but beautiful morning John put on a clean woven covering that he had washed and hung in the sun to dry. It smelled of sun and air. On top of it he put his camel's hair robe. It was the same morning that Daemon decided not to chase the vandals. They would eventually return, he knew. If he quit chasing them, maybe they would no longer smell his presence and would return to their old grounds. So when John picked up the staff that his friends had given him and started down the hill, Daemon followed. At a distance. He did not want John to know, and strangely now, he did not want John upset with him. Whereas at first he hadn't cared. In fact, he would have welcomed a fight. Now he wanted to be at peace with John but only with John. He had watched him from the first night and had seen that John was not angry or tense like the Romans, nor was he fearful or obsequious like the conquered people, bowing and scraping to obtain favors. This was the first human Daemon had admired. He knew now that John meant what he said. He was honest and unafraid. Even when the cat knocked him down he had had the presence of mind to find a rock and retaliate. He hadn't trembled then, nor even when the vandals surrounded the campsite. He had returned with the food and firewood in the dark, and Daemon knew that he would not know fear and always speak the same message that his body was broadcasting through its stance and its pores to Daemon or anyone else. There would be no discrepancy between thought and speech. Daemon had never given allegiance to any human, but with this one he was sorely tempted. Even if this one said that chasing the field animals was bad, he might give up this favorite sport. Not right now, but maybe after a while.

When Daemon came out of the wooded area into the clearing, he could see that John was already speaking to the crowds that were waiting to cross to the other side. There were women in the group and even some children, but John appeared to be speaking even to them. When he paused, they clapped their hands and shouted "good," and "yes" and "tell it like it is" even "glory to God" such as he had heard in the amphitheater when the emperor appeared. The boatmen appeared a bit surly as they waited to ferry the people across, not interested in John's water game, but wanting to get as many silver coins in a day as possible. Daemon could tell so much by watching the body language of these people, their gestures, their head carriage and the way they used their bodies, up straight or bending slightly and tense. But today, most who entered the water appeared relieved after they came out. They drew themselves up straight like people who had just dropped their heavy burdens of produce at the scales to be weighed and sold.

Daemon lay in the bushes under the small tree where he had lain before. It grew hotter and hotter but the weather seemed not to bother John. Of course, he was in the water up to his waist now, dousing the people. On the bank Daemon could see the two men who had come so often to the cave. They were signaling to John and trying to get his attention. When he looked their way they pointed to another man in a white robe walking on the shore with a few men following him. Daemon perked up his ears and was all attention. Wafting towards him was this man's pedigree shown through his body movements. Unbelievable! Here was another, like John, who knew no fear. Daemon watched his eyes take in the whole scene before him and seem to digest what he saw, like a shepherd who reads the entire flock of sheep and knows their next movements. He was fairly tall, not as tall as John, but about the same age with a softer beard and well-formed legs and arms, even perfect as of a Roman statue. Even more than with John there was something of authority about him. Was he the conquered people's emperor? He certainly commanded attention. He had a grace in walking. He planted his staff with ease. He had such assurance about him that he did not hesitate to walk through this huge gathering without first checking it out. When he arrived at the water, he went to where the conquered people were undressing to enter. He took off his robe, put down his branch and waded in. One by one those already in the water turned their heads, saw him and backed out, like pack members acknowledging a leader's first rights. Then, together with the others watching on the river's bank, they stood wet and shivering, neglecting to dress, as they waited John's reaction.

Daemon had never before seen John hesitate. He always knew what to do and no man or woman seemed to confuse or amaze him. But this man caused him to stop still; he dropped his pot from which he poured water over the humans and it floated next to him, slowly sinking. Then he bowed his head to the man entering the water and said something in a very reverent tone. The assured man smiled, reached into the water and pulled out the pot offering it to John. They spoke together for a moment and then John accepted the pot. He pushed the man under the water. The assured man squatted easily, much like a gymnast in the amphitheater, then rose surefooted and stood while John poured a pot full of water over his head. At that moment the gathered crowd, those already dunked into the river and those half-clothed and waiting, gave a huge sigh, altogether, much like the amphitheater crowd after the emperor pardoned a favorite fighter. Up above the sky split and threw jagged beams of light upon the crowd. A heavy voice Daemon could not smell said something, but Daemon could not even decide from whence it came. The humans in the crowd sighed again as one, but no one stirred. Except a bird. It hovered over the head of the assured one. Did it see his hair as a nest? Or pickings to pull and use in a nest? Suddenly Daemon wanted to catch the bird and pull it away. He didn't know why, but why didn't matter because Daemon couldn't move. He was immobilized like the assembled humans. He surprised himself by whining instead. Whining was something he only did in his sleep. It showed humility and submission, and it was foreign to him.[*]

The assured one came out of the water and put his clothes back on. Daemon watched as he went over to John who had followed him out of the water. He spoke softly to John and then hugged him. Daemon wondered if they were litter mates. They smelled similar. They had similar strong features, much like all the conquered people, but perhaps straighter and stronger. One difference was that this one had an ease at the corners of his mouth and in his eyes that John lacked. He spoke to no one else and no one spoke to him. Then he walked off toward the fishermen and got into the boat they had come in. His long hair lay

---

[*] *for event seen through human eyes – p. 219*

wet upon his robe. He did not look back and they rowed him across the river toward the other side, the side from which the sun fell. The gathered people stared and pointed after him. Even the ferrymen had stopped grumbling and waited silently. Soon they all knew that John was not going to tell them all they wanted to know about this man.

He had indicated that he was unworthy before this man and after some prodding, he gave them a name: "His name," he said, "is Jesus." They had never seen such submission from John who criticized anyone boldly, even a ruler he saw as breaking the law. John was a man who, like Daemon, did not back down. Daemon had seen that with the cat and with himself. What was different about this assured one that John so respected him and submitted to him? Was he John's pack leader? And if he was, why did they not travel together?

John nodded to the crowd; then he gathered the two waiting men who always came to visit and some others and walked off up the hill. It was obvious that John would not go back into the water today. Daemon saw the weak man, who had spilled his produce, blink his eyes in surprise. Then, like many others he slumped in disappointment that John was leaving. Those who had disrobed squirmed back into their clothes, the water glistening on their bodies making it more difficult to do so. But they were silent. The first to speak were those selling food for the crowd. Now they would have fewer buyers with John gone. They complained loudly, but John was out of range of their tongues. It was like the vandals out of Daemon's reach.

Daemon rose from under the tree. He ran down to the river and drank long full draughts of the water. The beach was all but abandoned now and the only activity was the ferry which carried people to the other side. He wanted to find out more about this Jesus, but the boat was no longer in sight and Daemon could not find his scent in the water. Some scent remained on the shore where his bare feet had walked, but it stopped at the water line and he could not pick it up. He had lost this man the way he lost Taursus. In the water. Daemon stretched, then turned around and headed back toward the hill and John's cave.

As the days passed Daemon became more and more interested in John. Every morning when the sun was up John would leave his cave and walk to the river where once again he would push humans one by one into the water. As usual he would talk to them earnestly and with authority. He would not eat until evening when he would bring back to the cave over his shoulder a sack with edibles. He would build a fire and meet with men who came to see him. Daemon noticed a change in John when he spoke with the men. He would take out his paste papers and use his finger on one spot or the other. The men appeared to not agree with John, but slowly they appeared to accept what he was saying and would nod reluctantly.

Daemon too was slow to accept John's word. At first he would growl and bristle at any new one coming up the hill, but John would come out of the cave, check out the arrival and say that one word, "back." Only once did John not use the word. That time it was two dirty half-clothed, youngish men who smelled like the sour drink Taursus used. Daemon had come from his pad and challenged them with relish. His lip curled back, his teeth glistening, his feet planted so as to be ready to spring, he snarled, and they half fell and half ran backwards down the hill.

Daemon waited for the order to "kill," but it never came. However, like the vandals, they were impressed. Those men disappeared and thereafter never returned, nor even any like them. Strangely enough, Daemon felt no frustration at foregoing the attack. Daemon surprised himself; like John with the bird, he had used just the needed amount of force.

Days and weeks went by. The group of men still came every night to the cave and Daemon relaxed because now he knew John wanted them there. One night, as usual, they were talking. But then they began shouting. The air was tense, and he was on alert. The men were arguing with John. Was it about Daemon? Did they want John to chase him off or kill him? Or was it about the assured one? By this time he had known his name, "Jesus," because he heard it that first time from John on the river, and many times since from the pack members at the cave. Jesus had been to the river again, but again he had left in a boat and Daemon could not follow. Daemon stretched his legs on the ground, clawing closer to watch the group. Then he saw one, the short one, take a long stick, walk around the front of the cave to the side where Daemon slept and with it pick up the animal skin that Daemon slept on. He brought it back towards the cave, careful not to let it touch him. There was a fire that John was making outside the cave and the short man seemed about to toss the skin into that fire. Daemon saw his muscles tense as he began to lift it. Then John put himself between the fire and the man and waved him back. In fact, John said "Back." Just as he did to Daemon. The man was upset. His skin warmed until it looked like the fishermen's faces the first day they took the summer sun. "Just take it back," John said, more gently. "I have told you that he saved my life. He has never entered the cave. He causes me no trouble. In fact, he probably saved me yesterday from troublemakers who climbed up here." John reached down and took a chicken from a sack. "Here," he told the short man, "put this by his pad, and come back in with us. We will continue our talk about my cousin from Nazareth."

The short man's face contorted; his body stiffened, but he reached out and took the bird. He walked slowly back to Daemon's pad with the chicken in one hand and the stick with the animal skin in the other. Once or twice he tensed and hesitated, and Daemon thought he might drop them both and walk away. He had seen his own kind, when angered and shamed like this; he had seen them walk away with their tails low, doing as ordered, but refusing to look at the human who was disciplining them. This man dropped both the animal skin and the chicken on the ground under the overhanging rock where Daemon stayed. As he walked slowly back to the group, Daemon heard John's voice. He was expecting him to berate the short man. In a Roman camp the soldiers would have been laughing and joking, even poking their chastised companion in his ribs.

"Thanks, Andrew," was all John said as he extended his hand to the returning man. Andrew took it and the men then all continued talking and cooking as if nothing had happened. It was all very peaceful, and puzzling. Daemon realized that John saw no threat in this Andrew, and he began to see a strength in John that did not rely on weapons. His strength was inside him, and when he spoke his voice resonated and pierced the stillness. Inside the cave it even echoed. What was it that gave him this confidence? He was afraid of neither man nor beast. Daemon had not been afraid either. But he had his strong teeth and jaws, legs of iron and fearsome sounds that rolled and tumbled from his insides. He had tricks and feints that had helped in the amphitheater. He had cunning which helped him overcome every opponent. He could be disobedient and not be discovered. What did John have? Did he pay these men to agree with him? He had never seen John take out a purse and give coins to other humans as the Romans did to their soldier pack members. In fact, with these men it was the opposite. They often brought John food and oil and sticks for his fire. All they received was to listen to him speak.

They carried no weapons. Yet they all carried those peeled branches. If it came to a fight, would they use them to pummel and maul their opponents? Would they use them to protect John? Right now all he saw was that the male humans leaned on them coming up or down the hill. Maybe there was something about those branches he had missed. They had never been left outside the cave so he could never inspect them closely.

As he lay watching, a picture of another large stick with a knob at the top came back to him. It was the one he had recently discovered and then abandoned. In his mind's eye the fight with the cat came into view. At the time he hadn't paid much attention to anything other than holding on to the animal's throat and clamping down with his strong jaws until he pushed through the sinews and veins and felt the warm blood on his nose and in his mouth and until the throbbing ceased. But now, now that he looked at the straight peeled branches resting upright in the firelight against a cave wall, he recalled a branch that had tumbled from John's grasp when the cat landed. That evening when John returned with the cooked fowl and the small branches to build a fire, John had not carried that branch.

Daemon began to put all his memory pictures together. His second image was that of John scraping with his foot under the bush, looking for something. Of course, the branch.

Suddenly, because that branch was important to John, Daemon wanted to get it. He wanted to press his nose against its smooth surface and pull the odor deeply into his nostrils and then exhale and pull in even more air from over the branch so as to identify it always with John. Even more, he wanted to touch his nose lightly to some bare skin of John's. For the last two mornings when John emerged from the cave, he wanted to run up to him and touch him. He was ready to acknowledge John as his pack leader. So far John only gave him the "back" signal. Maybe this branch would help. Maybe if he brought it to John and laid it at his feet, John would rejoice and let Daemon touch him.

Sadly, he suspected that touching John and making him his pack leader might not happen. Even if he delivered the branch. But if he retrieved the large branch that had fallen from John's grasp he might learn from it more about John. Who was he? Was he a relative of the man he had doused with water, the man whose head the bird had explored when the sky lit up? Could he find something more of John from smelling it. Could he tell where John had been? Would Jesus have been there too? Would there still linger on it something to tell Daemon more?

CHAPTER X

Abduction

He wanted to find the branch, but he was reluctant to leave the cave site. He did not know why. Something inside was warning him to stay, trying to hold him down. As if something bad was going to happen. He looked over at the cave. Now the men were singing together. The two who were always with John took leave of him and started down the hill as the light started to fade. The others replenished the fire and sat singing in voices that blended together. It was all peaceful. They would not hurt John. Daemon went back to his pad and tried to sleep. The moon lit the earth, almost as bright as day, but it was what was inside him that kept him awake. "Let it be," he told himself still holding in his head the image of the branch. But he couldn't. Whining softly he left the cave site and started down the hill and towards the site where the cat had attacked. Every few steps toward his destination he paused, turned his large head to the side and looked backwards. These motions slowed him down.

Many days and nights had passed since the incident with the cat. Several heavy rains also. When Daemon came to the spot where he had fought and where John had built the fires, he could find no residue, even of the cat. He nosed through the underbrush surrounding the clearing. Then he sat with his nose in the air, letting the soft breezes enter and searching them for some trace. He found none.

He sat on his strong heavy haunches, puzzling what to do. He was tempted to return to the camp and check on it. He was still uneasy about leaving. While he was debating, into his mind's eye came a picture of the soldiers he had followed. He remembered their searching habits. How they had walked and crawled in circles over hills to find their quarry, especially the time they sought the deserter. Finding him had taken them longer than it did to polish their spears and clean their gear, but eventually they found him lying under the lip of dirt that bordered a creek. The deserter wanted to fight them, but they shackled him and dragged him behind their beasts of burden over rough terrain back to the camp, terrorized and abused him, and finally stabbed him to death slowly, everyone getting a turn with his short sword, avoiding the deserter's most vulnerable spots until he was almost gone and until his voice was almost gone and he could scream no more. Then the head Roman stabbed him through his heart. They didn't dig a hole and put his body in it; they set him on a rock atop a hill where Daemon knew he would swell and burst and the vandals would claim his remains.

He thought again about the men who came to the cave. They didn't even wear swords. They would not kill like the Romans. He just knew it. When they caught a fowl they didn't tease and torment it before they killed it, watching it run desperately in circles. They simply slit its neck and drained the blood. The kill was simple and clean, not tormenting, as his chase of the small field animals. Daemon let the two killing methods drift through his head. The residual atmosphere after both killings differed as night from day. Both resulted in a dead animal.

But back in the camp when the soldiers finished their killing, he would avoid them as much as possible. They would strut and snarl and throw things around the campgrounds as if killing wasn't enough. He stayed out of their way so as to avoid becoming a butt of their jokes, or having urns thrown at him, or sour stuff dumped on his head. They extended their tormenting long into the night, waking any sleeping companions to join them (or perhaps to prevent their sleep). They always acted as if calmness and kindness were weakness they had to prove they had no part in. Yet John wasn't weak, and Jesus wasn't weak; both were calm and secure without such strutting. Daemon could not express it, but somehow he saw that not torturing a kill made those two humans something stronger than the Romans. They had more self assurance. It was as if they were cooperating in some plan they both followed and admired. He didn't want to believe this because once again he was pulling away from violence, anger and deceit and it scared him. He had already given up his chasing of the small field animals. He no longer growled at every female human and showed his teeth even though he did stiffen and raise his hackles. Wasn't that enough? What next? What if John told him not to attack someone who was attacking John or Jesus? He doubted he could hold back his anger. He needed John alive. He might want him as his pack leader. He was eager to fight for him.

Two questions began nagging him. "Would John ever be his pack leader?"

His second question: "Why did this man feed him yet would not touch him?"

Even Taursus would occasionally pat him on the rump after a particularly good kill. It wasn't affection, but it was like a shared triumph. Taursus shared because Daemon was property he was in charge of. But though John spoke sparingly to him, none of the men who came to the cave ever spoke to him, and none of them ever touched him. He didn't sense that they were afraid of him. It was more as if he was beneath them, even more beneath them than were the slaves in the amphitheater, as unclean as a dead and rotting animal, the kind he rolled in until Taursus stopped him with the almost hanging. Maybe John would pat him on the rump if he returned the branch. He didn't know why he wanted a pat. He had never particularly liked being patted by the Romans. Why did he want that from John? Or at least an affectionate word. He had never had affection, nor even wanted it. He would certainly never give it. He became more and more confused. He had decided a long time ago that he would never submit to another human. But could he live in a pack with this human and not submit? Now he did some things John approved of, but only some of them. He sensed that to be a part of this man, John, he would have to change in other ways, but he also sensed that no matter how hard he tried, no matter if he changed completely, he could never be fully accepted into the cave. John did not want to be his pack leader. If John could assure his safety and that of a recipient, he probably would try to send him away with someone who would feed him. John had no affection for him. What he had was gratitude and probably respect. Respect was what he got from Taursus, though he always knew that could change. He finally realized with a sinking heart that he need not fear submitting to John because John would never want his submission.

Soon he came to where he had seen the branch and began circling, searching for it. He moved quickly back and forth, sniffing his own prior trail again and again as he moved down the hill. When he was almost to the small creek he detected the faintest odor of John. He came upon a branch lying with its base under a big bush. He barely detected the odor, but the bush had kept it partially dry and thus it partially retained it. He gingerly pulled it through the weeds until he had it free of its entanglements. It was a large branch, its bark stripped. Still shiny as something that had been rained upon. It was longer than John was tall, and as Daemon moved up the hill he worked hard at pulling it free of one bush only to have it get stuck in another. When it stuck, it jarred his teeth and made him angry. He wanted to get back to the cave, but he could not get it to move more quickly.

So he worked it slowly back up the hill until he was in sight of the cave. He heard voices coming from the cave, but they were not the voices of John's usual visitors. They were rude and commanding. He felt his skin tingle and the hair on his back rise. Then he saw a few beasts of burden, not quite like the animals the Romans rode at the front of their columns, but beasts someone rode on. They snorted and pawed the ground when they saw him emerge from the wood. The feeling he had before he left to look for the branch intensified: all was not well; John's well-being was threatened. He dropped the branch and ran to the cave entrance.

Four men were in the cave with John. Two of them had John's hands behind his back and were tying a rope. One had his foot raised and set upon John's buttocks as he pulled the rope tight. John stood straight and tall and in his strongest voice reprimanded them. Even when John had told Daemon to stay back and out of the cave, he had not sounded so forceful. Daemon's eyes narrowed. His teeth bared. The hair on his back rose from ears to tail. And his tail, catching the anger, swept low and back and forth. These men were attacking. He braced to hurl himself into the cave. Then in Daemon's head the memory of John's command, "Out!" resounded like a siren. He had never entered the cave; so he hesitated now, out of habit. But just for a moment.

But in a battle situation a moment lost can be disaster. It was here. One of the men who had taken John's new staff swung at that moment and the staff crashed into Daemon's head. Soundlessly he whirled on wobbly legs and dived at the human's legs. At the same time, from the corner of his eye he saw a second man pick up a rock, which had cooled from its place around the fire, and throw it at his stomach. He dodged it, but it caught his hind leg just as he sank his teeth into the boot of the man with the staff. At the same time that he felt his leg collapse, he ground his teeth into the boot. The man yowled in pain much the way the victims of the Romans did while being crucified. But even though Daemon moved his rear swiftly and swung his legs low to protect them, as he did in the amphitheater, the others who had left their prisoner, picked up whatever they could find and bombarded Daemon with rocks, with John's flask of oil, his new branch and his cooking pots.

In a short time he was unable to move his limbs from the pounding and his eyes clouded with fog so that he could no longer see clearly, but he hung on to his catch with his large, unforgiving jaws. He was through the tough animal skin of the boot and beginning to taste the salt of that man's blood. He knew that he would never let go; even in death his jaws would clasp this human's leg. His catch was by this time flat on the floor, yelping with pain. Then John spoke:

"I will have him release your partner in crime, if you promise not to further harm the dog." The man on the ground yelled "Yes, please yes," in agony. Two of the men who had their rocks raised to throw brought them back to waist level. John then looked at Daemon: "Enough," he said. "Back. There is no way that you can save me from this fate. For this I was born. They have come from the Tetrarch, and they will take me to him. I only wish that you could tell my disciples where I have gone."

Daemon was confused. He was willing to die in this fight. As in the amphitheater he would never surrender. But though John had not wanted any power over him, he respected John. And so, reluctantly, he released his hold. His jaws ached as he withdrew. He could not move any other body part because of his broken bones. He tried, but could not lift a paw. His sides stung as he breathed and he tasted some of his own blood in his mouth mixed with that of his catch. One of the men raised his arm again to use a rock. He was still afraid of this pounded dog. He stayed many feet away though he must have known that Daemon could not get to him.

Then they all heard it. Sounds coming up the trail. Human voices. They looked at each other. "Never mind the rock," one yelled. "That dog's already gone. Get one of those donkeys in here." So the man dropped the rock and brought one of the outside beasts of burden into the cave and they lifted the man with the bloody leg onto his back. When they did, the man screamed, and then they stuffed something into his mouth to stop his noise, though they did nothing at all to silence John. They all mounted the beasts. The largest beast had to carry one of them and John as well. As they trotted off a different way than they had come, John looked back at Daemon, but Daemon was silent. He made no sound. He was dying.[*]

Daemon heard the men as they came into the clearing in front of the cave. The short man was there and he could smell him. He smelled others who had come to visit, but he could not see any of them because of the veil over his eyes. He knew he was broken all over. His legs would not move except for one which moved in the hip socket, but would not change position because he was lying on that side, and if he tried to move off the hip, he felt each of his broken ribs. Never before had he been beaten in a fight. Never, even when Taursus had hung him, had he felt pain like this. Even breathing was painful. As he pulled in air, he could feel the blood rise up in his throat from deep in his lungs. He was breathing in short gasps. He did not fear death, but he regretted not winning the fight. If he had ignored John's "back" command ringing in his memory, and if he had entered the cave, he could have easily raced from one to the other of the men who took John. He could have slashed one's arm, run up another's back to bite his neck, probably chased one to make him run off and mount a burden beast and gallop away. All would have ended well. But he had, for the first time in his life, without threat hanging over his head, been obedient and followed the orders of another despite his own contrary feelings. Now what would happen to John? If these men were like the Romans, they would take him somewhere and kill him for their pleasure. Maybe even have a fighter dog or two

---

[*] *for event seen through human eyes – p. 219*

rip him. Why did he not fight? He was young and strong and together they could have easily defeated those men. Why did he not carry weapons? Did he think that his voice was so important that it was all he needed to persuade? Who did he think would respect a man crying out in the wilderness?

These memories raced through Daemon's head. As he grew weaker, his anger began to subside. He was resigned to death. It was part of life, and so when he pulled in, with all his remaining strength his last hoarse breath, he felt it rumble through his chest in arcs of diminishing pain and then he relaxed. At least the vandals would not dispatch him, but only rip and fight over his remains.

Even as he stopped breathing Daemon's awareness went on. In his head and in all his being he felt a presence walking up to him as he lay on the edge of the cave. It stopped beside him. He had little sniffing ability left, but he knew it was Jesus, the one who had come to the river and spoken to John. Daemon knew from his smell that he was one of the conquered people and yet, through the cloud of pain and his loss of energy, he recognized a strength in this man he had never felt even from the large animals with the tusks and huge stomping feet. Not even from John. Then suddenly, and surprisingly, he felt a warm outstretched palm on his side. And the warmth radiated as from a push on the center of an anthill, carrying its healing messengers into every part of him. First his ribs shook slowly and as they used to do when he stood up from sleeping, they stretched until they settled back in place. Underneath the side he was lying on he stretched his unbroken leg without pain. His three broken legs mended their joints into place, even the one with the smashed foot and bleeding toe nails. They became fit.

Then cautiously he moved his neck and the pain was gone. He blinked the blood from his eyes. He spat a mouthful of blood and mucous and swallowed slowly as his breath returned. Just as slowly he manouevered his body into a sitting position. He stood up so easily that he sat back down from the surprise. Jesus was standing there just looking at him. Daemon understood now the tremendous power of Jesus. If Jesus could restore his broken, pounded body, he could cure anybody.

Daemon stood again and whined and wagged his tail freely and with gratitude. He had done that only once before, as a very small puppy, but the person who elicited that happiness had then taken him from his mother and dumped him unceremoniously into a pen with three older pups that sniffed him and sniffed him until he was exhausted. Soon he had stopped wagging his tail. He stopped wagging it now as Jesus walked away.

Daemon watched as the five men who came with Jesus gathered up John's scant belongings, the little leather rolls he sometimes wore on his head, his plant papers from the cave, his cooking utensils, an extra piece of clothing. They placed them on the cave floor before Jesus who was now seated on the rock that John sat on to read his paste pages. Daemon watched Jesus carefully. He did not respond to the others any more than he had to Daemon. He did not lean down to touch John's possessions with his nose as Daemon would have done. He just put his face into his hands and rested his head so that his long hair hid his face. He remained that way a long time. It was as if he was no longer with them, but was somewhere else with someone else.

Daemon sat on the periphery of the cave a long time and waited a signal to trail and look for John. But it was as if these friends of John had forgotten him. Would they go after the marauders? They had no beasts to ride, but they did have Daemon. With his sniffing ability he could find where they had taken John. He stood strong and stiff legged. His body responded better and stronger than it ever had. His muscles bulged eagerly to begin a search. He looked to Jesus for a signal to follow after the marauders, but Jesus gave none. Instead, disappointingly, he motioned to the men to pick up John's possessions and follow him and he started west toward the river, not to the southeast on John's trail. It was getting dark. Daemon was confused. Daemon knew that this Jesus was stronger than the stampeding amphitheater beasts, that he had more power than the huge cats and the bears he remembered from two years ago. He was stronger than the man who sat in the amphitheater with a crown of leaves on his head deciding who would live and who would die. Never had Daemon found anyone with such power who was unwilling to use it. Surely someone who pulled back Daemon's breath and unkinked his legs and ribs could wither those marauders and bring John back!

Why did he not do it?

CHAPTER XI

Indecision

Daemon was disappointed that Jesus' group did not follow John's captors. He did not know where to go next, or with whom.

Daemon had stayed with Taursus so as to eventually get revenge for his almost hanging; he had planned to turn on Taursus and slash him and live up to the name they gave him in the amphitheater. He would attack when Taursus showed fear. But he never did. He had sung while overturning the boat.

Daemon saw in John another who would never show fear. He knew that even if those men mistreated John or put him in the amphitheater with fighter dogs, bears and hunters, John would not scream and cry in fear. Neither would Jesus. Even if the Romans attached John or Jesus to a cross, neither would show fear. It was strange. Daemon had seen many men who were strong and hard, but nailing them to a cross made then weaker than women. Especially if they hung there many days and nights. He felt that John and Jesus were alike. But why? Did they know things no one else knew? Were they unafraid because of a connection to something or someone else that he could not see but could feel. Did this attachment to something or someone else make them strong and unafraid? Daemon shook his head trying to clear the debris.

Taursus had given Daemon many orders. John had given only two: "back," and "out." Jesus had given none and had even touched him. Jesus was of the conquered people, yet he had touched him.

Taursus enjoyed the evil Daemon did. They enjoyed it together: terrifying little field animals, chasing women who came from the well with water pots on their heads and laughing when they fell and the pots shattered into large shards. Taursus gave orders to kill a certain man, woman, or child and it was as if he himself plunged into the stomach of the living human with Daemon, he so much enjoyed the kill. They both did. They encouraged each other in evil. But for Daemon, the best thing about living with Taursus was that Taursus never knew the tricks Daemon played on him. Taursus would have killed him had he known. But he never knew, nor even suspected until the very end how deceitful Daemon could be. And then it was too late.

John on the other hand didn't ask anything of Daemon. Daemon got used to not doing what John disliked. He got used to not chasing the little field animals down by the river. He knew that John would be disturbed if he chased them away from their shepherds. John did not believe in terror, not even in chasing the women who came to the river. When Daemon growled at them, John looked sharply his way. So Daemon avoided the animals and the women, resting high above the water under a large bush. He did not do what John would not like. And he surprised himself in that he was not deceitful about it. He was still tempted to sneak into the cave when John left, but as time went by, it bothered him less and he found himself content with his place outside. John never thanked Daemon for his restraint, nor asked him to follow him. What bothered Daemon was that he knew that John would be just as pleased if he left his spot outside the cave and never returned. John did not want him as part of his pack. Inside Daemon felt the same kind of hurt he felt as a puppy at being dumped. John had treated him better than any in the amphitheater and any of the soldiers he traveled with. After his time with John he was content not to terrorize the little animals. He didn't growl and snarl at the men who came to visit John, nor at the women and children at the river. He never even deceived John. Still, despite all his efforts, John did not want him around.

Daemon felt emotions he had never felt before. He felt obedient to the point of not doing what John did not like and leaving off deceits. However, something was missing. It was something intangible and the humans had given him no word to name it. He knew "Back" and "Down" and "Kill," "Eat" and "Stay" and "Out." He knew "Taursus" and "John" and "Jesus" and now John's short disciple, "Andrew," who tried to chase him off. But he had no word for this emptiness and longing deep inside. It was there even when his hunger and thirst were sated. It never went totally away. As his head cleared he began to realize that he had not been born as a loner. He needed a connection. Even in the amphitheater he had been part of a pack, a pack that terrorized together. Wouldn't he somehow need a pack now? He thought of the mangy curs outside the large city wall. It was tempting to search for, find, and lead them.

For the next few days he sniffed distractedly around the cave. He kept picking up tiny fragments that fell from

John's skin and that of his captors as they bound him. Thus he registered his memories of John. He also picked up the smells of Jesus and retraced his steps outside the cave. His smell was strong and vibrant. Every step he had put down was deliberate and unhesitating. After each round of sniffing, Daemon drank at a spring near the cave, but he did not eat. He did not trace the steps of the animals of burden, or even the blood drops from the foot of the man he had bitten. For some reason that he did not understand he was reluctant to look for John. It had to do with Jesus. It was his hesitation that puzzled Daemon. It was as if Jesus knew that John was not coming back. And as if Jesus agreed with that, even though Daemon had felt his sadness as he held his head in his hands. But he knew now for certain that Jesus was not going to use his power to help John. Did his own failure to act independently of Jesus mean that Daemon was following Jesus? If not, then why did he not search by himself? He did not need this Jesus to search for John. He had a better nose than Jesus. Still he did nothing.

As days turned into weeks, a heavy sadness, like a pounding steady rain, settled on Daemon. Every day he smelled every rock, every bush, every pathway, outside the cave for the fading smells of men and beasts of burden. Every day he wandered through the area and down to the river bank. Every night, exhausted, he slept in his old nest beside the cave where he had trod down a second weedy patch for his body. He ate fish that he caught in the streams and any small animal which ran across his path. But gone was the wish to torment the small animals as had been his pleasure in the past. He missed John, but he had never had him as a leader. Perhaps he missed Jesus more. He could not forget the touch of Jesus, the warm feel of his palm on his ribs. It left an indelible mark. In fact three times he had passed a decaying animal and not rolled in its essence because he did not want to disturb the place where Jesus had touched him. Oh, yes, he remembered how on past occasions he had twisted his body supinely as he dove into such matter, pushing his shoulder and ear artfully at an angle so as to absorb as much as possible. Sometimes he even rubbed into the excrement of a large or small animal. To deceive Taursus he would afterwards roll in the sand and swim in a creek or river until the smell was much reduced. Then he would torment a small animal, kill it and bring it to Taursus who would mistake Daemon's foul odor for that of his catch.

One night, a night not too far from when all the conquered people took to the roads to go up to the city where Taursus had once left him to wait outside the gates, Daemon woke with a start. His body swelled. He urinated before he was fully upright, sloshing some of the urine on his hind legs as he rose. And then he defecated on the cover that John had put down for him. He continued until his insides felt entirely empty. Instinctively he knew what had happened: John had died. Daemon knew that in a powerful, absolute way. John was now like the animals slaughtered and bled by the conquered people themselves, not by the Romans. A sacrifice. John was the second man he had followed. He had followed two men halfheartedly. Both had fed him. The second had respected him, and Daemon had returned that respect. Both male humans had died violently. Would this happen to any human he followed?

What about the third man, Jesus? Despite his healing, despite the power of it, Daemon was reluctant to follow Jesus. Not because Jesus too might die. But rather because he sensed that Jesus would ask too much of him. Not just to give up his freedom to chase and scare and be devious about his deeds. Maybe even to accept the weak ones, to let the women and children and weak men come near him. Maybe even to let them touch him. Surely that was too much to ask. Those humans were weak and fearful and he disdained them and had still to rein in his desire to attack every time they came near. Yet Daemon shivered with emotion when memories of Jesus warmed his brain. He saw Jesus in the water with John, and at the cave with the other men, and even more than these sights he felt on his ribs that warm, extended, healing hand. That hand that had never again sought him out.

So much of what Daemon knew came from somewhere inside him. Daemon didn't study the dried plant sheets as John did, or understand the words yelled at him by persons who were frightened of him on the beach. But he could tell a human's or animal's intentions by his or her breathing, walking, smell, the way he held his body, his motions. He was very good at reading an approaching human or animal and that creature's intent to ignore him, fight him, or try to cow him. He knew instinctively that this Jesus also received information from the inside.

Daemon whined. Not a whine of fright, but of confusion. He turned round and chased his tail. He ran up to the cave and back down into the weeds from which he used to watch John's evening meetings and smell the roasting of small, grazing animal flesh. The smells were mostly subdued now, like weeds after winter when only a very faint dust of odor remains. Outside the cave time and rain had mostly worn away the smells of the captors, the horses and the blood of the wounded one. The only smell still recognizable was that of Jesus.

Daemon put his shoulder to the ground and wallowed in that smell. Then, drawn in some inexorable way, maybe just because he could, he turned and followed the footsteps of Jesus.

CHAPTER XII

Destination

Those footsteps took him to the river and the ferry that had brought followers to John. They stopped at the river bank where Jesus had stood with two others. They did not continue on Daemon's side of the river though Daemon worked his way north on the landing, then south smelling for another trace. He still found none. He sat perplexed. Then methodically he followed the river south for a few miles, but met no Jesus smell, not even a stale one. He drank at the river. He would not eat until he found what he was seeking. Finally he started north on the east side of the river and as he walked determinedly along, a breeze wafted his first smell of Jesus. Jesus and his followers had crossed the river.

Daemon went down to the water and put one foot in, but the water rose on his leg chilling him. The memories of that long ago, near-death experience with Taursus raided his mind. He whined and tried again. For a whole morning he stayed at the water's edge, sometimes plunging in until the water reached his stomach. Always pulling back. He even tried to swim, lifting his legs and curving them, moving in circles. But finally he pulled back for the last time. Lifting his head, he resumed his search for Jesus by inhaling and testing the air floating toward him from the opposite bank.

He walked to the north and beside the water until again he identified human smells. Romans. On this side of the water. They were fairly fresh and many. They were on the sand, the rocky ledges, the trampled grass. They went down to the river where they trailed onto flat tree pieces suspended over the water. Those tree pieces were supported by more tree pieces, hollowed out, such as some used for fishing. The whole apparatus was roped together and bounced and jostled on the water, moving the entire two-tiered contraption up and down and sideways. Obviously, from the smell of it and the smells wafting from the opposite bank, the Romans had marched across this thing which spanned the water and landed on the other side.

There was no one in sight on either side. The sun warmed his skin. He drank again. He walked to one side of the thing the Romans built, then the other. Each time that the lapping water would lift it, he would jump back. Then again Jesus' smell wafted toward him. That did it. Jumping squarely forward he landed a few feet onto the top tier. He felt a sliding response beneath him and slinked down, tensing his legs and clawing stiffly to crawl slowly toward the center. He heard the lapping waves on either side of him and knew he was over a running waterway that slapped and struggled to take down this human creation and the canine on it. He felt, rather than saw, one of the hollowed-out pieces break free from the rest and felt the river quickly fill that opening. He scrambled all four feet together and, crouching low, ran the remaining distance to the opposite bank. When he looked back, the apparatus was still on the water, still together, but pulling to one side. Soon it would drift down the river as had Taursus.

With new energy he picked up the Jesus scent. As he cantered on, the tall plants with bright flowers, those with strong perfume that almost obliterated the traces of Jesus, and the tiny dark-flowered plants brushed his legs. Toward evening the land grew more hilly. Large stretches of flat land, but interspersed with hills. That first night, after he caught a small brown animal that had played dead in his path (silly not to know that Daemon had eaten many dead ones), he climbed up to a cave in the hillside. He scraped a circle with his front feet at its entrance and slept there until morning. That morning, after a short run, he found he was near a city. He smelled the footprints. They went into the city, and it became clear to Daemon that Jesus was still travelling with others. The smells that were faint in the cave were stronger here. Maybe even Andrew's. Their steps went both toward the city and away from it, and so he put his large nose to the ground and inhaled and let the information travel around inside until he identified the departing footsteps as the stronger. So he knew that Jesus had come back out of the city and was headed to higher country. The smell of the humans he was following told him that all those he had identified the day before were still walking with Jesus. But here there were others as well. Did they come from the city Jesus just left? They had no other meet-up tracks; so Daemon decided that they had come from the city. He followed, and following became easier as the group grew. That night he again left the trail and climbed up to a cave and slept.

On the third day he proceeded more slowly. The land became much more hilly and rocky, with rocks the color of creamy bird eggs. But many, many times that size. The ground was a similar color. As he passed the caves on the hillside, he saw more and more creatures: those with long slim horns which took to the highest hills, those with flat tails which dived into the creeks and rivers when Daemon appeared. Even some cats like the one he had killed so many, many days ago. Daemon ignored them all and they ignored him, even the cats, although a small one jumped into a tree as he passed and snarled and scratched. Daemon gave it a wide berth though he assessed its power as much less than his own. He could probably defeat it, but he was not to be sidetracked – now that he was onto a trail.

Late that same day he came to a large lake. He pushed through the tall, thick, stick-like growth that surrounded it. As he shook his shoulders free and advanced, he felt something cool and wet creep between his toes. He was in the water. He pulled back quickly, fearful; he knew what water could do. It had killed Taursus and almost killed him. He sat down backwards pressing beneath him a cluster of prickly growth. Yet he did not leave. The smell of swimming creatures tempted him. So he crouched and cautiously pushed forward. He pawed at the water. He drank mouthfuls. But he did not enter. Just as he prepared for a full retreat, from the corner of his eye he saw movement. He leaped and grabbed as the creature entered his air space. Stretched out, sinewy and wet, he felt its heart beating as it filled his mouth. He knew then it was one of those creatures that croaked in the night. He shook it fiercely, breaking its back and splattering water onto the shore to make dark wet spots upon the sand. He finally feasted.

The sky told Daemon that the day was coming to an end. There was a slight breeze coming from the lake and more humans were passing on a road above the water. Daemon avoided the humans. In fact, he waited until almost dark to take up the trail again. It went around the lake, through a very dry and sandy area, and then back into a land where lush fruits and vegetables grew. Many medium-sized trees, round, like bushes on sticks, held their tiny green fruits. Nearby them their grandfather and grandmother trees still grew and flowered and budded into fruit. Further on tall trees with leaves like bird feathers made a roof for travelers on the road and also bloomed into flowers and fruit.

Jesus and his group had walked here. In the morning after a short nap with his body curved into a circle, Daemon woke and drank from a spring that trailed into the large body of water he feasted beside the day before. Then he followed the steps once more on the road until they again entered a town. But although they had entered the town days ago, no tracks showed they had come back out. At least not on this side of the town.

Daemon debated whether to enter the town. He knew that the townspeople would not want him there. Late at night they closed and locked their doors to keep out the curs that roamed the streets and ate dead animals and garbage and would fight with anyone brave enough to wander about alone. Unlike the Romans, the conquered people did not allow dogs in their nests. Only the field animals, usually those which gave milk, or those with the long ears that carried the burdens, were allowed in the nests at the lowest level. Daemon had seen them on one of Taursus' excursions of terror. Of course, when he was with the Roman soldiers, he did not have to honor any of the wishes of the townspeople. He could simply flaunt his power just as Taursus did.

But today he was on his own. And so he proceeded cautiously, creeping from the shade of one stone nest to another. Sometimes enjoying the shade from the overhanging dried growth on the roofs. He knew that the conquered people used this dried growth to cover their nests and feed and bed down their field animals. He had not gotten very far along when he realized that the town was deserted. At least this part of it. He saw no one. And so he began to walk more boldly.

Soon he heard a murmur ahead, like many flying animals gathered on the beach and preparing for flight. Up ahead he could see humans pushing and shoving, some trying to puff themselves up and make themselves look larger as Daemon did when preparing for a fight. They surrounded a nest and Daemon knew from the trail that Jesus was in that nest. He sat down very quietly under a tree which covered him with shade and he knew that if he remained as still as when he hunted, the humans would not notice him. They kept milling about; suddenly started shouting and pointing. Daemon looked and saw some of them up on the roof reaching down, others lifting up to them a human on a sleeping mat until they brought him up on the roof. And then Daemon, lifting his nose high and inhaling, smelled the Jesus smell rising from inside the nest and knew that it came through a large gaping hole in the roof, like the ones the Romans tore into the conquered people's huts to terrorize. Into that hole they lowered the human. Daemon watched and waited. Gradually the milling crowd quieted. They were quiet a short time, and then they drew back from the front entrance of the home, leaving an open pathway through which came a man carrying a mat. Daemon recognized the smell of him. It was the man lowered through the roof. He was happy, skipping and dancing and singing. He raised his legs high and bent his knees as he literally hopped like the tall birds that chased little creatures through the water. Daemon wondered if he had been stung by one of the flying creatures that provided the sticky liquid; so energetic were his movements! Not likely. He was too happy to have been hurt. This had to do with Jesus. But he didn't stay with Jesus. Instead, the roof man ran off with one of the men who had lowered him through the roof. His other helpers stayed.[*]

Daemon continued his watch under the tree. Once he tried to move closer, but a woman shrieked when she saw him, and soon the waiting men picked up stones and threw them at him. The stones fell short of Daemon, but he decided not to approach. Instead he took a measure of them and knew that if he wanted to get through the crowd, all he had to do was to rush at them and they would make a pathway for him and yell and scream as they fled out of his way and dropped their stones. The men at the amphitheater had fled; all he had done was look at them. But once inside, what would Jesus do? Would he send him back out?

As the shadows lengthened, the gathered crowd thinned. Even some of the humans inside the nest came out and hurried away. Jesus did not come out. Nor his friends who had visited John with him and the others whose footsteps Daemon smelled in his travelling. They stayed. Soon the area outside the home was empty. As Daemon crept slowly closer, a large wooden door was rolled over the open pathway into the nest to block entrance. The sound of happy, tired voices and the smell of cooking came through the hole in the roof and reminded Daemon of John's gatherings. Except at John's gatherings Daemon received dinner. He was not shut out without food as he was here.

[*] *for event seen through human eyes – p. 219*

Daemon was hungry and he knew he would have to leave his watching post to find his dinner. Throughout the whole afternoon the only animal he had seen was a small roundish one which emerged from a hole in the ground. He trotted over to the hole now and with both feet scratched at the hole until it was deep as the first joint on his leg and round enough to hold his sitting form. But the animal was gone; then he saw it watching him from another hill not far away. Angrily he rushed upon it, but missed as it dived down another hole. He started scratching away, but stopped before he worked too hard. There a few feet away was the small animal watching him again. This time he ignored it. Instead he used his nose to identify the smell. He would keep that memory present and work to find it coming up through the hole. He would grab it before it had a chance to retreat. And so, he walked away, observing many holes in between the grasses and bushes. He listened carefully and heard the messages being sent above and below the tunnels. Now there were a few of the animals watching him from their perches next to the holes. None came up near him. None was going to be dinner. Nonetheless, with no other food offered, he sat quietly waiting.

When in the deepening darkness he could see simply the outlines of hills and trees fingered by the moon, he left the area and climbed up into the hills. As he strode through the rocks and weeds, he disturbed a nesting bird which he grabbed by its foot as it took flight. Pulling it down he held it with one paw while he bit it fiercely to break its neck. Then he took it and carried it down the hill to eat within sight of the nest he had watched all day. The blood ran warm and soothing. The stomach contained grain not as yet digested, but edible nonetheless with the organ meat he extracted by shaking his head to loosen it. When he finished his meal, he licked the blood from his heavy paws and stretched. He heard sounds coming from the town, but they were animal sounds and he ignored them. Instead, he lay with his face between his outstretched paws, dozing until sunrise.

CHAPTER XIII

Solamen

Returning to the town the next morning, Daemon sat under the tree and watched humans bring their farm animals outside. Other humans with large staffs and pieces of wood with which they made bird sounds, led the animals out to grasslands. Women with large jars on their heads walked together toward the middle of town. The nest in which Jesus lay, stayed still. Close to when the sun was overhead someone emerged with a large milk animal and two young. He walked on the same path as the others. Jesus walked out soon after with a human that Daemon had seen carrying large bags of clinking metal pieces. This morning he had none with him. From the respectful way that he turned his body to Jesus and listened he seemed to have chosen Jesus as his leader.

Daemon was glad that Jesus was still accepting pack members, but if Jesus was like John, Daemon would not be one of them. Daemon would approach Jesus to see. Just then, a woman, returning with a full water jar, saw Jesus. She set down her jar and ran to greet him. Soon other returning women joined her and then the men who had not yet left for the olive groves and the fields. A huge crowd enveloped Jesus and like the raging river swallowed him from Daemon's sight. All that was

117

discernible was a large circle of water jars heating in the sun.

Daemon had no way to meet with Jesus alone that day. Humans who lived in the town brought their weak members, those whom Daemon despised: the pale, crippled, blind, those stunted in growth. All those who should have been dumped in a bucket and drowned at birth. He did not know what Jesus did when he met a weak one, but he knew there was power coming out from him. When Jesus touched a weak one, Daemon saw a powerful change in that human. But besides what he saw, Daemon's own body reacted to that power. He felt as if it were being pumped full with air to all its boundaries and beyond. It was most uncomfortable. He had trouble breathing and his head spun so that the crowd rode up and down in the air like a heavy cloud from earth to sky. Daemon whined and rubbed his eyes on both sides with his heavy paws. This happened time after time. Nowhere, and from no one but Jesus, had Daemon felt such power. It wasn't like a soldier's power. That was all outside of him. This was from Jesus' inside. When Jesus touched and healed someone, it made Daemon's own side tingle where Jesus hand had touched him. It made him somehow feel akin to those pale, crippled, blind and stunted, as if they were all his litter mates. That made him angry, and yet he was thrilled at the same time. Unable to sort his feelings, he walked unsteadily away.

He went up a little way, back to the ground-animal holes. He settled under a tree from which he could watch three separate holes. For a very long time he neither heard, nor saw, activity. Then, almost next to his tail he felt a very slight movement of the ground. A little roundish animal emerged. Daemon remained motionless until it stood on its hind feet, twirled its head, and then darted a leg's distance toward another hole. At that moment Daemon pounced from behind and caught the round animal in his jaws. It wasn't much to eat, but what a satisfaction to know he could catch it. He needed to feel his own power.

All day long from where he lay he saw humans come to the nest where Jesus stayed. There were always humans surrounding the nest, three and four deep, like those who filled the cheap standing area of the amphitheater. Even at the time when most humans rested, in the heat of the day, the humans stayed around the nest. Towards evening Jesus and his new pack member came out. Jesus said something to the crowd in a gentle voice, but he seemed to have something planned and he walked briskly away and up the dusty road until they came to another, larger nest. He went in, but the crowd seemed less comfortable, and only a few stragglers followed. Only Jesus' usual group, some from John and some new, went in with him. From the outskirts where Daemon walked, he smelled the cooking, the roasting animals, the simmering vegetables and pieces of dried plant coming from the nest. He saw women enter with large trays of field produce that they had cracked open and sliced into pieces. Men came too. They had servants with them who carried the sour drink that Taursus always had. They wore coverings with glittering trims. On their arrival someone else washed their feet, and they left their footwear both inside and outside. Torches were lit outside as early evening came on. With the day's crowd dispersed, inside the nest the humans were celebrating with Jesus and his friends. Daemon could hear their merrymaking.

Again that evening he had no way to see Jesus alone. He snoozed beside a wall upon which vines with small flowers grew. When the moon was high in the sky Jesus finally appeared, put on his shoes and walked with his first group, those who pulled fish from the waters. He went to the nest he had stayed in before. He took off his shoes and entered with three of the humans. Daemon went back to the post where he had slept the night before. He was determined to meet Jesus alone. He lay with his large head facing the door to the nest and was alert to every scurrying sound in the night. Each time he woke and peered at the closed door, he closed his eyes again in disappointment.

Day after day played out the same scenario. Daemon watched for Jesus. Jesus was surrounded with humans. He had an unbelievably large pack filled with all types of humans: men, women, even children. Mostly conquered people, but now and then, a Roman whom Daemon identified from his smell and the metal plates on his wrists or legs. One listening Roman, who rode a field animal, was clearly not a pack member, but a leader. And still the crowd grew. Every day Jesus spoke to them and laid his hands on certain ones as he had on Daemon.

Daemon stayed out of the way – "back" as John had told him, but from that stand-back position he could feel anger in the hearts of some watchers. Surely Jesus was the leader of the pack, but there were those who hated him. Daemon felt their desire to pull him down and destroy him so that they could then lead the pack. They whispered to each other from the edges of the crowd. Usually they wore coverings with trims that reflected the sun's rays and their foot coverings were bright as if recently cleaned, their heads crowned with many dangling bits of leather encasing the dried plant pieces. Their eyes flashed. Their limbs were taut and ready for a fight. Sometimes they asked questions of Jesus, and when he answered, they left, kicking pebbles or spitting words into the dusty road. Daemon watched them carefully. He waited for Jesus to order that harsh Roman command: "kill!" It never came. So he moved around restlessly rubbing his back against a tree stump and scratching a new spot in the ground to sit. When the angry ones moved off, he finally settled down.

One morning, before the sun's rays could reach all the corners of the yard, Jesus emerged from the nest with three of his pack followers. They began to walk swiftly toward the mountain. Daemon followed happily thinking that at last he would have his chance to approach Jesus. But as they turned the corner on the dusty road, a human shouted at them. He shouted a question and Jesus answered. With that the human ran back toward the town, blowing a horn cut from the head of a mountain creature. And as the foursome, with Jesus leading, ascended the mountain, they were soon joined by others. Humans ran carrying their foot wrappings, holding their belts, and with their faces still encased in sleep, tripping on the road. The one who had blown the horn continued to blow it. Daemon knew that he was declaring the way. The Romans did that as they advanced into battle.

By the time that Jesus and the three others had climbed halfway up the mountain, many people were with him. Not many old. Not many infirm. But many humans, men and women, who had left their daily chores to follow him. Daemon could tell from Jesus' slumped form that he was very tired. The way Daemon felt after a long hunt. Jesus sighed a long sigh. But then he looked at all his followers and he smiled, opened his arms and motioned for them to come and sit beside him. As he sat halfway up the mountain and talked to them, Daemon could feel a change come over the crowd. They had followed Jesus like desperate ants on a food hunt. But now they sat contentedly, some with their backs against boulders, others using their backs like posts for their pack friends to lean against. They were there a long time and Jesus spoke to them as if he had so much to tell that he had to make sure he told them all of it this day. Once in a while the whole group would sigh and make a sound like "ahmen," as if agreeing with Jesus. Many cried into their body coverings and splashed eye water down their cheeks as they listened. Daemon would feel their submission to this Jesus and the power they let him exert over them. None of the jealous ones with their glittering, shifting eyes had climbed up the mountain, and so the gathering had none of the tension as at the nest.

As the sun fell Jesus stood and spoke to the crowd. He gestured toward the top of the mountain and as they rose to go with him, he held up his hand, palm open and fingers spread. The "back" signal. He was going to ascend by himself. One of the women rose and went to him from the back of the crowd. She took his hand and appeared to entreat him to do something. He simply hugged her and then shook his head, kissed her and set off for the mountain by himself.

Daemon circled far from the crowd and up the mountain to intersect the path taken by Jesus. As he went, he pulled in air over his whiskers and into his nostrils. He could smell the tracks of the winged creatures, the little furry ones and the flesh eaters. In particular, the tracks of three of the flesh eaters kept crossing the path he had made. He was disturbed. Then he knew why. These were the same curs that he had met outside the big city's gate. But he did not smell the tracks of the large shaggy one, their leader.

These three must have tracked him here from where he had crossed the river and through the many days he had shadowed Jesus. He was angry to realize their skill. He was angry he had missed them. He was tempted to turn back and confront them, but he kept following Jesus instead. Until he realized that the three curs, with the strength of their tracking skill, were now ahead of him and after Jesus. Had he identified a vulnerable prey for them and put them on Jesus' trail? Were they hoping to pull him down? Would Jesus be their meal for the day? Quite an easy one. The attackers might not even need for one of them to spring on Jesus' back; the odds were not in Jesus' favor. Daemon tried to sort his own feelings. Why should it bother him? He had wanted to get close to Jesus. But judging from Jesus' constant avoidance of a meeting, Jesus wasn't wanting to get close to Daemon.

When he reached the summit, Jesus sat on the ground in the open, pulled up his knees and placed his back against a tree. His branch lay beside him and Daemon could see him relax and immediately fall asleep. Soon his soft, regular breathing and some bird calls were the only noises to be heard. Soon he heard a soft rustle above him on the path, close to the summit of the hill. Then more vibrations going toward Jesus.

Daemon made his appearance, running ahead into the clearing. Immediately he heard their communications: soft growls, a soft whimpering. Then once again the only sounds were the bird calls and Jesus' soft breaths.

Daemon emitted a low growl, and the curs that had regrouped, walked through the bushes toward him, strategically placing themselves so that he could not attack more than one at a time. But though they did come cautiously, their approach was not challenging. None tried to circle behind him. They knew who he was. They followed him because of his win in the long-ago encounter outside the city wall. When he did not charge, but merely brought his height to its fullest and waited, two of them came forward with muted sounds of greeting. Then they inched up, slowly but eagerly, to be next to him. Daemon knew that they wanted him as their leader. Whatever had happened to the brown shaggy one? Why had these curs left the large city? For how long had they been trailing him? This he did not know. But he let them come forward and he smelled each one. His whole body tingled . . . until he realized that the third cur was slinking away toward Jesus. His stance told Daemon that he was going to attack Jesus. Jesus would be their meal tonight. Most humans had more sense than to walk these hills alone. There were large cats out here much more dangerous than the curs, but a lone human was easy prey for either. Now with Daemon here it would be short work to take down Jesus.

Daemon was hungry. He was looking for a connection, a pack. He was surprised to find that he really was not a lone animal. As nasty and dreadful as it had been under the amphitheater, and despite his feelings of superiority over all the other fighter dogs, there had been a connection there. Perhaps a shared purpose, evil though it was.

Daemon began sensing that this Jesus who had cured him might become his pack leader. This Jesus had power that Daemon could not understand, but could feel. But this Jesus seemed unwilling to notice him, not to want him for a member of his pack. Had the small man who used to visit John, but who now followed Jesus, convinced Jesus not to allow Daemon near him? As Daemon stood hesitating whether to join the pack in the kill, Jesus woke and saw the third cur coming swiftly from the bushes. Daemon stepped away from the other two. With a low growl that came from deep inside him he sprang with all his might from the edge of the bushes. And landed squarely on top of the cur. The cur saw that he had overstepped. He knew that it was Daemon's choice to make a kill if Daemon was to be his leader. And so, with a yipe he slid from under Daemon and tumbled part way down the hill, his scrawny legs digging straight trenches in the soft dirt. The other two followed swiftly.

Daemon stood on all four, large, strong feet and looked at Jesus. Jesus looked back. And when he did, Daemon saw that Jesus loved him. His side where Jesus had touched it, warmed as if fingered by the morning sun. A new kind of energy surged from that spot, a channeled energy, not like the boisterous overload which always invaded his being when Jesus cured a weak one. Each cure of that kind had flooded him where he lay with a dizzying, full, puffy swelling that left him breathless and uncomfortable almost to bursting.

But this new energy was strong and personal. It entered his body like rain water streaming through a dry and parched creek bed. This was an energy that darted forth into the channels and inlets of his body, rounding itself sideways, upward and downward. It bounded through his heart, his legs and shoulders and up through his head with a delicious freshness which made him shudder and roll over in the dirt onto his back. Upside down, his tongue lolling out, he squirmed happily next to Jesus despite any lingering memories of past rejections. Then legs in the air, chest and stomach exposed, he lay still panting softly. He

125

was the picture of perfect submission, a submission he had never given anyone before and never thought he would. He always thought he would rather die, be torn apart in the amphitheater, be stabbed by soldiers, or even crucified. He always thought he would never submit to animal or human, yet here he was down before this Jesus. Flat on his back.

Jesus reached out to Daemon and Daemon, dusty and attentive, rose, shook himself and moved near. He could not get enough of Jesus. When he touched Jesus with his broad wet nose, Jesus laughed and taking him behind both ears pulled him closer. Then Jesus scratched his ears and under his massive chin. Finally, Jesus put his arms around Daemon and held him tight. He hugged Daemon and said very clearly: "Henceforth I will call you 'Solamen' because holding you on this mountain and rubbing your warm body comforts and consoles me."

Jesus turned Solamen's head toward his own, and with his beautiful dark eyes he gazed affectionately into Solamen's own shining orbs. "You are abandoning your old ways. When you came upon me tonight, not only did you resist the temptation to slash and tear and do evil, but instead you brought me solace. Never before have you submitted to anyone. Not to the Romans. Not to John. But for me, with an open heart, you have put yourself on the ground.

Solamen whined happily. He tucked his large broad snout into Jesus' sleeve and felt the warm flesh inside. Such happiness he had never known. His being ached with happiness until . . .

Someone was coming up the trail with a torch lighting the way in the gathering darkness. Jesus stood, and as he did so, Solamen slid from his grasp and sat before him, adoring him with large, liquid eyes. Then Jesus motioned Solamen away. In fact, he gave the same, hand-outstretched, "back" signal Solamen hated. But automatically and sadly Solamen retreated to the bushes. Unnoticed, the curs had vanished. Undoubtedly hunting another victim.

Soon three humans appeared: the short one, another that smelled like the short one's litter mate, and the woman whom Jesus had kissed before he ascended the hill. The short one, leaning on his stick with one hand, carried with the other hand two sticks, one with fire atop; the woman came next, easily and almost musically placing her walking stick; finally followed the last human carrying a stone container with a lid from which escaped smells of vegetable and fish. Jesus greeted them warmly. He hugged each one, but lingered longest with the woman. He spoke to her with the warmth he had shown Solamen. She was tall and graceful. She walked with the same astonishing ease as Jesus, easily avoiding the stones and vines that entangled the path. At first Solamen thought she might be like one of the many conquered women he had seen the soldiers bring late at night and push screaming into their tent. A woman for Jesus. But when the wind came from behind her and his whiskers sought out and screened her smells, she had none of the body odors such as came from the Romans' captives at such times. In fact, the woman had a sweet and clean smell that showed the opposite: an absence of fear and stress. None of the three visitors had any body odors like those which seeped from the Roman tents as the soldiers did their partying.

They sat in a circle with Jesus until the moon came full into the heavens. No one ate of the food they had brought and finally they hugged again and left. But not before they had lit a torch for Jesus and placed it into a hole they dug. And not before the woman approached him and with a quizzical look slowly removed some small pieces of something from his robe and dropped them on a large flat stone. She said nothing to Jesus about what she had done, but again kissed him tenderly. And Solamen saw that they looked quite alike. In fact, if she would swell larger and have Jesus' face hair, she could be a second Jesus. Their features were quite similar, even the way they moved their bodies, their gestures, the warmth toward others. Then Solamen knew: this was the female human who had borne Jesus, and nursed him with her body. Unlike Solamen, who had been torn from his mother, Jesus had kept his and grown up with her. Unlike Solamen, Jesus did not despise the female humans. In fact, in the crowds which followed Jesus there were more each day. Solamen knew instinctively that if he were to follow Jesus, he would have to accept the female humans, or at least not show his disdain towards them. That would not be easy. Of one thing he was sure: he would never submit to a weak, female human. If he had not submitted to John, surely he would not submit to a woman.

Very late that night Solamen left the bushes and walked slowly back toward Jesus. He paused and put his nose on the rock that held whatever it was the woman had removed from Jesus' robe. To his astonishment he found five of his straight black hairs. Of course, he could not ask Jesus why they had been taken from his robe. Once Jesus accepted him, he would have thought that Jesus would like to wear those hairs. He would like everyone to know that he had a huge, strong and ready fighting animal to protect him. From henceforth Jesus would not have to worry about going into the hills at night by himself; Solamen would go with him. As he approached, Jesus saw him come into the light and motioned him on. He touched Jesus with his nose and then sat beside Jesus and watched as Jesus ate from the container they had brought him. After Jesus had his fill, he turned over the container and spilled the remainder on the flat rock, avoiding the area on which his mother had placed the hairs. Solamen eagerly lapped up the pieces of swimming animal and cooked field vegetables not eaten by Jesus. As Jesus lay down on his cloak, Solamen licked the last juice from the stone and then, no longer restless, he lay down content at the feet of Jesus. He had found his leader.

CHAPTER XIV

Acceptance?

But the next day his adored leader showed a puzzling side. Coming down the mountain he gave Solamen the "back" signal. He walked ahead until he came to the shore from which he had dismissed the crowd. There he met the short man and enough pack members to fill two boats. For that is what they did. They walked to the large water, piled into the boats and crossed to the other side. Solamen remembered his last trial in the water and shuddered. The water had been fierce and as determined to kill him as the huge, tusked animals in the amphitheater. He whined as he watched the boats move away from him across the water. From inside the boats he could hear human voices joined together in song like the birds, but heavy, masculine and all on the same notes. He splashed one foot into the water. Then he shuddered. He cringed and withdrew quickly from the peaceful water. He was afraid. He was losing Jesus, but with all his might he could not force himself into that water to follow him. Soon Jesus' boats disappeared from his sight. At the same time a large furry animal, running from something or someone, passed close to his legs. Releasing all his pent up energy in one thrust, he reached down and punctured its back with his large teeth. He vigorously shook the animal until he cracked its neck. He carried it in his teeth back to a safe place to eat for the humans were coming to the beach at that time, speaking Jesus' name and apparently looking for him. Maybe the animal had been running from them. It was a gift like the extra rations thrown him after an amphitheater kill.

Solamen waited all day for Jesus. As the heat increased he moved further back into the bushes. Humans came too during the day, and all appeared to feel the same disappointment as Solamen at the loss of Jesus. Toward evening, when there were no longer any humans searching for him, when the beach was deserted, Jesus returned. He walked slowly and Solamen stood up to approach him. Happily he ran through the weeds toward Jesus. But when Jesus saw him, he paused, a short pause that the humans probably did not notice, and he spread his fingers and raised his hand as high as his waist in the "back" signal. Solamen came to a quick stop, spraying clods of dirt as he slid. With a few others Jesus walked off to the town and the nest he used before, and Solamen slept again on the hillside.

Solamen lay there many days, just watching Jesus, his every move. Each night, after the sun fell, Jesus and his pack would enter a nest and not come back out until morning. Outside the home the only sign of his presence would be some few, carefully-placed, side-by-side foot coverings as well as many others tossed in a heap. That heap looked like one built by a group of young humans run off to play. Some nights, if there were no humans outside waiting and watching for Jesus, Solamen would play his own game. He would creep up to the pile and search with his large wet nose until he found those belonging to Jesus. He would pull the first Jesus' one from the pile and push his huge head and shoulder into it. He would fill his nostrils with the smell of those sweaty feet and from the clinging grains of sand he would discover all the places Jesus had been that day. Then, if the area was still safe, he would find and scoot the second covering over to the first, lie down with both between his paws, and pull the Jesus smell deep into his being. The next morning as he lay back watching the followers emerge from the nest with Jesus, he would enjoy their puzzlement at finding Jesus' foot coverings aside from the others. Jesus would only smile as he put them on.

Solamen became aware that Jesus had a very large following, filled with humans of all kinds, including: those who truly wanted to follow him; those who were there simply to get something free; and those treacherous ones, waiting as he had with Taursus, just waiting for a time and place to destroy Jesus. He read their body language.

Then there were those, including female humans, who brought food and provided shelter for Jesus and were part of his really close group of followers. Solamen began to identify these close ones as Jesus' pack because Jesus always took them into the nest with him at night. Over and over he saw the two who had visited John, the short one who did not like Solamen and his pack mate. Then there were those who drew the swimming creatures from the lake, and the one who had played with the metal pieces. One very young one, who seemed very close to Jesus, walked beside him a lot. Sometimes he stayed in the nest where they had all gathered. Early on, one sunny day, that one's mother had come for him and pulled him aside from those climbing into the boats with Jesus. She pointed to Jesus and shook her head vigorously and held out her hand to her son. Solamen recognized from her tight body language that she wanted him to leave Jesus and go with her. He had memories of that same kind of messaging that pleaded that an offspring was too young to leave the nest. His own mother had been reluctant to let him go. But John, for Solamen soon recognized his name (puzzled that it was the same name as that of the one who pushed others under the water), ignored her outstretched hand, and then with a dreamy, distracted look, hugged her resistant body and took off running to join Jesus and the others.

When Solamen smelled the air coming from around a certain tight-skinned one, he identified an eagerness to follow, but also touches of anger and confusion. His body, even after a long day, did not relax as the others. It was as if he was always alert, always ready for a hunt. Never relaxed.

One night when Jesus came outside the nest, Solamen started to approach him, but the tight-skinned one was right behind Jesus and spoke to him. Solamen knew he wanted something of Jesus who listened to him, then called out a name: "Matthew." Outside to join them came the one who played with the metal pieces. It was a rare moment when there were no lingering second-string followers loitering nearby. This metal-pieces player, this Matthew, listened to the tight-skinned one, but seemed reluctant to agree. He turned to Jesus, giving his back to the speaker. Jesus listened, but then spoke softly to Matthew until Matthew nodded his head. While the tight-skinned one stood silently watching, his tense body spoke a strident message: "I want control." Jesus then held out his hand to Matthew who reached into his covering and handed Jesus a bag clinking with metal pieces. Obviously there were things more important to Jesus than the metal pieces. Solamen growled softly when Jesus handed that bag to the tight-skinned one. He watched as Jesus embraced them both and sent them back into the nest.

Solamen sneaked closer. With a soft whine he told Jesus he was behind the hole from which the humans drew water. Jesus came over and sat on the rock ledge surrounding the hole. Solamen scrunched beside him into the cool rock and against Jesus' dangling, swinging leg. He rubbed his body there against the rock and against Jesus' leg, softly moving it back and forth to a slower rhythm. Feeling the lack of Jesus' usual peacefulness, he softly pushed under Jesus' hand with the plane of his massive, thickly-haired dark head. Jesus responded by reaching down and scratching Solamen behind the ears. Slowly Jesus' body released its tension. His foot quit moving of itself and offered no resistance to Solamen's leg massage. As Jesus began to relax, Solamen knew that Jesus would like to have Solamen with him more. He did really comfort Jesus. He did not understand why he had to be kept away. But he had become a pack member. Like the female followers who were not always allowed near Jesus, he would obey.

Larger and larger crowds came to listen to Jesus. Often angry word fights broke out among the few dissenters on the outskirts, and sometimes one of them would boldly push his way until he was right in front of Jesus. There he would do the angry human bark, the "a-hem!" to get Jesus' attention. Always, Jesus speaking straight to the challenger, would give him an answer that left him speechless; so that he departed like a defeated fighter dog with his tail between his legs. Jesus then continued speaking to those who were honestly seeking to be his pack members. More and more female humans came with their male humans, and sometimes even by themselves, or with a weak and ailing offspring for Jesus to touch. He always did. And somehow the male or female young one was cured.

Each time Jesus touched one, Solamen felt the swelling in his own body, filling it like a flooding river to its utmost boundaries and beyond. Often Jesus' release of energy made him dizzy, and it only dissipated slowly.

One morning just before dawn, Jesus and his pack members came out of the nest with their walking sticks. They wore sacks over their shoulders and they were eating pieces of fruit, the size of small bird bodies. They were laughing and jostling each other as they took to the dusty road. Solamen followed. They stopped at the spring, washed their hands and drank deeply. Jesus drank first, but after all had finished, he poured water into the scooped-out, hard vegetable they had dipped into the water, and leaving it full, he set it on the ground. For Solamen? Solamen drank thirstily, sloshing the water over his large teeth and full cheeks until it dripped and dribbled down leaving a damp spot on the ground.

They walked until the sun was overhead. They came to a town shining in that sun. Unlike their last town, it was busy with many male humans doing many things. Many carts stacked with things made by the humans. Many carts with food. Many male humans on the shore of the big water dragging in the swimming creatures to sell to others. The nests here were larger than the last town. Big pieces of the stuff mountains were made of were piled atop each other. The people had cut them to fit each other. In fact, Solamen could smell the dust of the mountain stuff being chiseled in another section of the town.

A few humans had followed Jesus and his pack, and now, as they rested under some trees heavy with little fruits, these humans caught up. They asked something of Jesus and he responded by speaking to them. He was much more relaxed today. His speech was happy and gentle and the people gobbled it up like flying creatures flocking together over grain.

That night it was hard for Solamen to find a place to sleep. He had to move beyond the borders of Jesus' new sleeping place to avoid the dogs that prowled through the streets at night. After a few restless hours he moved to the seashore and found an abandoned shed where people exchanged metal pieces during the day. Cramming his rump into a tight space and with his forepaws and head hanging through the opening he managed a bit of restless sleep. As he lay inviting sleep in the uncomfortable nest, he pictured all the animals who had sleeping places. He saw the holes made by the little ones he had so much trouble catching, those who moved so quickly during the day and had many resting places. He saw the large nests of dried vegetation above him in the trees where the winged animals rested, and in the foothills he passed the warm, smelly dens of the animals with the long bushy tails. Most of the humans also had places of their own. At the end of the day they did not have to hunt for resting places. They had their own. Then a memory of Jesus, walking the roads, dusty and sometimes as hungry as Solamen, came into his brain. And he knew that, like himself, like Solamen, Jesus too had no nesting place of his own. All of these humans who came to see him nested in stone nests or maybe in caves, but they all had their own places to rest at the end of their work. Not Jesus. He always used somebody else's nest. Was Solamen following a loser? Could a loser have such mighty powers to make the weak humans jump up from their carrying pieces and walk? Could a loser bring sound from a soundless one, or erase the putrid sores that marred skin, the kind of sores that also marred the skin of one of the curs? If Jesus was a loser, he was a mighty loser.

So, the next morning Solamen rose while it was still dark and trotted to the nest in which Jesus stayed. After a short wait Jesus came out with his pack members and started walking. Before he had gone very far a female human came out with two of his pack members. They had baskets of food which they showed to Jesus and his friends, and the main female human handed Jesus a small bag, which he in turn handed to the tight-skinned one. Solamen could feel that one's excitement as he took the bag and explored its depths with his fingers. Even from this distance Solamen knew that he would guard this bag. He walked far behind Jesus and the others, dropping it deep into the nesting place in his clothes where he kept his growing hoard of metal pieces. Solamen was soon close enough behind him to hear them clink together. The tight-skinned one continued fingering the metal pieces until he lagged so far behind the others that he had to run to catch up. As he ran, he looked guiltily to both sides and to the rear and caught sight of Solamen with his strong muscular legs easily loping behind him. Solamen saw that he was frightened, and so Solamen darted behind a stand of small bushes, stood perfectly still, and watched.

Jesus listened to the tight-skinned one's excited babbling and moved his eyes over the road they had come. While the tight-skinned one pulled on his sleeve and pointed toward Solamen's hiding place, Solamen felt Jesus' gaze as he acknowledged him with the slightest, imperceptible tilt of his head. Jesus was not worried about Solamen; his body language said that. Actually, Jesus' body quickly sent the message that he was a lot more comfortable being trailed by Solamen than by the angry ones who yelled and argued with him and always disturbed his peace. He patted the back of the tight-skinned one and told his followers something that made them laugh. Then Jesus took an animal skin bag from his shoulder and handed it to the tight-skinned one who kept staring back down the road. Solamen knew he was trying to locate him; but Solamen did not move. Finally the tight-skinned one drank from the skin and gave it back to Jesus. Jesus then took the bag over to a rock and emptied it.

It became harder to follow the group now. Because the tight-skinned one kept turning around and looking for Solamen, Solamen had to stay farther back and dart farther from the road. On the rock on which Jesus had emptied the skin, he found enough water to slake his thirst, for fortuitously the water had landed in a bowl-like depression which had no cracks to lead it back into the ground. The depression was almost exactly the depth of the depression in the head gear with which Taursus, when he remembered, or was reminded, used to water Solamen on the soldiers' marches.

Up ahead the group turned onto a road, and with their backs to the sun walked to the next town. Before they entered, Jesus took the only basket still full of food and set it on the ground behind a large stone. The short pack member picked up the basket. Another questioned him, but Jesus threw up his hands and gave a gesture that meant they should all leave, and the short one put the basket back down. They left. Jesus turned as they did, dropped his hand by his side with his fingers curled toward the food, and Solamen knew it was for him.

As soon as the group was out of sight, Solamen approached the stone, walked behind it and smelled the dried field-animal strips. He pulled one gently from the basket and over the straggly grass. Then he bit into it. He took it a few feet away to eat it. Then he looked around again cautiously and took another. And another. And another. He would not have been able to say "thank you" to Jesus but he would have licked his hand and wagged his tail in appreciation. Maybe, for a dog that was the best way to say "thank you."

As the group entered the next town, Solamen saw the townspeople come over to Jesus. In fact, Jesus' mother was there. Jesus shook hands with some, hugged and kissed others and then continued walking until he came to a large building. He sat down on a large rock and motioned for his pack members to sit beside him. There were beggars nearby and Jesus motioned to the tight-skinned one and pointed them out. Reluctantly, for Solamen read his movements, he stood, reached into his robe and withdrew the small animal skin with the metal pieces. He went over to the beggars and slowly and carefully with burning eyes looked each one from head to toe, demanding submission before handing out one of the metal pieces. The last one he jostled, as if by accident, and the human dropped his stick and took a few easy steps to the side. Thus, he showed himself not to be crippled, and he received no metal piece. The tight-skinned one yelled something derisively at him. Solamen matched this beggar's imbalance with the tight-skinned one's own interior instability. The similarity was so striking that Solamen wanted to separate the two of them from Jesus and into a rival pack. He simply had nothing but mistrust for the tight-skinned one.

Hearing the scolding, Jesus stopped speaking to his pack and called the tight-skinned one to him. Reluctantly (Solamen saw from the shift of his shoulders), he went over and sat with the others. They sat off the road in a little space under the trees with the many small fruits, and when the curious humans walked off the road toward them, Jesus motioned to the large building and directed them to it.

Then Jesus' pack members stood up, came over to him one by one, hugged him and started off back the way they had come. They went two by two. The last to leave was the young one. Solamen scrunched up through the weeds and watched Jesus hug him longer than the others. It was as if Jesus was sending him out on a first hunt. It was as if Jesus was concerned for the dangers that might attack this youth. But the youth was not concerned at all for himself. In fact, from his enthusiasm and the way he pulled away from Jesus, one would think he was a veteran of the amphitheater. He went with his litter mate, the oldest of the group, who seemed hesitant, who, as Solamen read him, would rather have stayed beside Jesus. After they left, the young one striding ahead of the older, Jesus gave Solamen the "back" signal and went into the building where so many men had gathered that others had to wait outside.

Jesus stayed in his mother's nest in that town. Very early in the morning the two of them would come out and walk before the first humans gathered. Even earlier, or late at night she would prepare food for him, and she watched as he would finish the food and then leave some on a rock beside the nest, for Solamen. One morning before they left, as she wound a covering about her head, she seemed to be asking Jesus a question. He pointed toward where

Solamen was resting. Then he gave Solamen the "come" signal with his fingers curving toward his wrist. As Solamen rose happily and approached, Jesus' mother stiffened and put her hand on Jesus' arm. Jesus then gave Solamen the "back" signal and leaned toward her and spoke until she relaxed. They spoke a few more minutes, and with one last glance at Solamen she retreated back into the nest. Finally, Jesus gave Solamen the "come" signal. Jesus' exchange with his mother had meant a long wait for Solamen. He had watched and survived that wait-down on all fours with his ears tight against his slightly-bowed head, his tail thumping mightily and his throat gathering spittle through his low, purring growl. Now with Jesus' mother gone inside, Solamen wriggled happily on his back under Jesus' touch. Solamen knew again that Jesus loved him, but that **only** Jesus loved him and that all the others wanted him to stay away.

Apparently the townsfolk wanted Jesus to stay away from this town as much as they all wanted Solamen to stay away. As Solamen watched from different hideouts, they argued with Jesus. They protected their territory. They challenged him; Solamen saw their bodies swell stiff and tall the way a challenging cur's would. They brought their sick to him, but even Solamen could tell that except for a few who did submit to Jesus' power, the others were more like wily curs ready to challenge whatever Jesus did in their territory. Solamen understood why Jesus did not cure all their sick as he had in other towns, why he could never be a pack leader for these humans. And so, one morning early Jesus left that town and returned to the one by the sea.

As Solamen walked away from that town in the footsteps of Jesus, the crowd behind him began growing again, now even pushing carts with sick and pallid ones whose hidden sores wafted their message to Solamen. Jesus stopped for every one of them.

Solamen knew instinctively that he would not be close to Jesus again until Jesus went to a place where the crowds could not follow. All he could do now was to track those footsteps, occasionally wriggling his nose with pleasure at their freshness. Mingled with Jesus' smells were some he had known a long time, some he had known from John.

When Jesus was near the town, he swerved off the road and followed a narrow trail to the large water. When he arrived at a small clearing on the bank, he was met by his pack members with boats. Jesus tripped slightly as he climbed into a boat, and Solamen saw that much of his energy had dissipated. Jesus was very, very tired. So he got into the boat with his followers and rested his head in his hands as they pulled away from the shore. The crowds arrived minutes later. They saw the boats out in deep water and knew, as a pack often did, that with the leader gone, there was nothing to hold them. They backtracked, upsetting two carts in their haste.

After they left, Solamen ran to the deserted shore and began following the far-off scent of his leader. The wind picked it up from the water-side and brought it to him in snatches. He inhaled. He pulled it in and ran a long way alongside the water before he again heard the sounds of humans ahead, and before he almost ran into them.

He found them gathering in a large area far from town where there were no man roads. Only trails. Here the cart handlers had had to push a way through the tangled weeds that lined the path, jerking and jostling the person in the cart. Others walked warily on the path, holding out their arms to sick ones walking beside them. None could push ahead because of the narrowness of the path. But once in the open they could advance freely.

As Solamen came upon them, he crept out of sight. Soon, though they looked tired and wind-blown, they began to cheer as with one voice. Solamen knew from the happy tension in their call that Jesus was almost there, somewhere really close ahead. Had Jesus been sleeping? And in his sleep revisiting events and experiences tucked deep in his memory? Solamen knew what that could be like. He had times in his sleep when he went back to the amphitheater, or he was with John, or times with Jesus like the touch on his side, or the time he had been re-named. And he knew that when he saw pictures in his sleep, he made funny, squeaky kinds of sounds and his legs jerked without his ordering them. Did Jesus twitch in his sleep? Sometimes those times back were wonderful; sometimes they were horrible. He raised his large black head, held it immobile, and slowly and carefully pulled in drafts of air to check what Jesus was feeling. But the wind was behind Solamen, blowing toward Jesus. Jesus could read him, but he could not read Jesus. So he watched for a sign as the pack pulled into the shore and the male humans waded into the water to grab onto the boats and drag them to shore. Jesus sprang out of a boat and greeted them, and Solamen knew he had been refreshed by a very short nap.

Because of all the gathering humans, Solamen had to move higher on the hill and behind a rock. He would have preferred staying close and guarding the space near Jesus so that Jesus would not get knocked down. He remembered the scene at the amphitheater when the watching humans climbed over the wall and tried to rush into the floor of the amphitheater. He had seen the other humans protect their young and pull them toward the exit, away from the excitement. He was ready to blast through this growing, excited mob to rescue and protect Jesus. He knew how to do it. He would growl and threaten with his large, sharp teeth. No one would come close to Jesus if he stood in the way.

But, as he watched, the youngest, close follower of Jesus took Jesus by the arm and moved back to the water and to a boat held there by the oldest one. With humans grasping for his robe in a way that brought a low angry growl from Solamen, Jesus stepped into the boat. Evading the many hands reaching for the side of the boat, the young one named John cheerfully pulled out into water too deep for the grasping humans to reach and threw a heavy metal anchor over the side.

Then Jesus spoke to the crowds. And they quieted as Solamen had, when as a pup he was offered his mother's warm, fragrant teat. When Jesus finished speaking, no one moved. He came back onto the shore and touched those in carts and those holding onto others. It was a cool day and the wind rose briskly, so that those who sat on their coverings, picked them up and threw them over their heads and shoulders. Jesus stayed until the sun slanted down and the animals that had carried the humans shifted restlessly. They were used to being bedded down at this time, tucked away and protected from wild animals. They were glad to leave.

More pack members who had gone out two by two came back tired and happy; so that now all the pack members were here with Jesus. Jesus greeted them and asked them questions. Finally, the one who had formerly counted metal pieces, handed Jesus a basket. The basket was like the one Jesus had left for Solamen. It had baked vegetable pieces called "bread," and a second basket, handed to Jesus by another human in the crowd, had some baked swimming animals. Holding up both baskets Jesus looked to the sky and said something that made Solamen's skin tingle from the tip of his nose all the way down through his tail. And he saw that the other animals, tethered off the path, shook themselves and stomped their feet excitedly. Then Jesus handed the baskets to his pack members and they passed them to the people. It was a happy, busy time as the humans reached into the baskets and withdrew as much as they wanted. The baskets never went completely empty. In fact, Solamen saw baskets, lying half-full, just moments before, now sitting by the path filled to the brim. These were grabbed up and passed quickly to the humans who sat far back so as not to worry them about getting a share. He remembered how the wild animals sometimes went hungry because there was not enough of the kill to satisfy them all. Then only the pack leader and the most powerful others ate. Today, this food satisfied them all until not only their stomachs were full, but Solamen felt the warmth of the Jesus' kindness within them. Jesus filled their hearts like no other.[*]

After they had all eaten, Jesus stood up and gave them the back signal. Many, who had been healed during his stay with them, came up to him and kissed his hands. Many came with water running down their faces and some dropped to their knees and kissed his dusty feet. All he did was to put his hands on their heads and whisper to each. With the very young ones who came up last he

[*] *for event seen through human eyes – p. 219*

would hold one or two against his chest as a few drops of water ran down his own cheeks. Finally all were gone and the pack members lifted the ropes to pull up the metal pieces which anchored the boats. They were ready to take Jesus with them. But he declined. Instead, keeping one basket of the leftover food, he handed them the other eleven and gave them the "back" signal too. When they had gone from sight, he gave the "come" signal and put the basket in the weeds for Solamen.

CHAPTER XV

Introduction

Solamen wanted the food, but he was too excited to eat. He was beside himself at having Jesus to himself. He had to release some of that emotion before he exploded!

He picked up an abandoned foot strap lying in the dust and tossed it into the air, catching it on the rebound. The second time that he tossed it, Jesus reached over and grabbed it from its flight. Solamen lifted his ears, set his front paws opposite Jesus, lifted his tail stiffly and barked. For the first time in his life he barked, not in warning, but in gladness. Jesus laughed. It was Jesus' own way of barking a response. Within the timbre of Jesus' bark Solamen felt a breakthrough into the good things of life he had so far ignored. Now in Jesus' voice he recognized and remembered bird song and slapping waves on the shore, breezes ruffling the little leaves, the bellow of a field animal at the call home for supper.

When the followers had left, Jesus' body had been lax with a certain edginess. Pretty much the way Solamen felt after hiding all day in many places. But now he felt smooth energy from Jesus again. His body stiffened like Solamen's. He held the strap teasingly high, though Solamen could have knocked him down and secured it. Instead he barked away, filling this deserted place with sound. And Jesus was his counterpoint, laughing freely. No one was there to hear, and that was what made it so good, so free. Then this re-energized Jesus threw the strap many paces away. It was a strong throw, over Solamen's head and far up the beach. Solamen ran to retrieve it. He dug his paws into the ground and spun to stop by the strap, sending sand particles high into the air. It was covered with his own spittle and with sand when he retrieved it. So he shook it grandly before he took it back to Jesus and dropped it at his feet. Jesus picked it up roughly. No concern for the sandy wetness. He threw it again. And again. It was the first time in his whole life that Solamen had played. It was the first time in a long time for Jesus.

Their game lasted a long time. When Jesus finally pocketed the strap toy, the moon was full in the sky. Solamen felt Jesus' body relax again but without the edginess it had had when the followers left. Solamen's body, by contrast, grew more eager to play. He would have played all night. All he wanted was more of Jesus. But it was late and Jesus patted Solamen's large head and began the climb up the mountain.

Solamen gobbled the food from the basket, drank quickly from the lake and followed the footprints of Jesus up a mountain. On that mountain Solamen knew that all the things he used to seek were not as important anymore. Being near to Jesus was. More than all the evil he had enjoyed, the slashing of weak humans, more than the deception and tricks he had played, more than leadership of a pack, food or drink, he wanted to be close to Jesus. He wanted to feel his touch. That alone was enough.

That night on the mountain Jesus allowed Solamen to squirm up to him and lie tightly beside him. He rubbed Solamen's belly, his ears and shoulders. Then, with Solamen still tightly against him, Jesus lay down on his cloak. He was quiet a long time though he was not sleeping. He seemed to be elsewhere, communicating somehow with someone or something else. He fell asleep for a little while and Solamen guarded his sleep. He had guarded humans before and would keep one eye open this night for vandals and other undesirables. If he saw a human coming, he would wake Jesus. Unlike the soldiers he had guarded with before, Jesus had no sword or spear. So Solamen was particularly watchful.

Toward morning Jesus woke, and with Solamen by his side he strode down the hill tapping his branch. He went so quickly that Solamen had to run to keep up. Through sleep Jesus had regained an enormous amount of energy. Solamen was proud to be his pack member. However, they were soon to be separated again. When they neared the water Jesus turned, leaned over and patted Solamen and rubbed his shoulders. Then he gave him the "back" signal and hurried down the remaining steps of the mountain.

Solamen watched Jesus as he reached the shoreline. The boat and the pack members were far out on the water and the wind had picked up. Solamen enjoyed the cool weather that was tossing the boat merrily up and down.

Jesus started into the water, but Solamen's eyes widened as he saw that Jesus was not sinking but walking on it, on top of the water as if it were sand. The pack members screamed across the water when they saw him coming. He spoke back and kept walking. It was misty out so that Solamen could barely identify the follower who climbed out of the boat to play on top of the water with Jesus. But when he fell in, Solamen knew from his scream who it was. It was the old one who always reacted swiftly. Too bad that he and Jesus had such a short play period before Jesus pulled him out of the water. Solamen would have stayed up on the water and played with Jesus as long as Jesus would.[*]

Solamen felt the tenseness in the hands coming from the boat to help Jesus transfer the soaking wet one into the rocking craft. Then Jesus vaulted into the boat and sat. The wind died at once and not a sound came across the water from the pack members. Not a sound. Solamen rubbed his face with his paws. This Jesus was different from any human he had ever known.

Solamen went down to the water and saw that the boat was barely visible now through the mists and waning moonlight. The sun was touching the tips of the trees with light. Solamen hesitated to follow. Again the memories of that long ago disaster with Taursus raided his mind. His second experience with the Roman contraption over the water had not been much better. He felt in charge only if he kept his legs on the bank. He would even dart to the water's edge and with his mouth reach in and catch a swimming water creature. But he could not, simply could not, plunge his legs into the water. His brain did funny things to him. It convinced him that his strong legs would not support him in the water. That he would lose control and sink below the top of the water and not come up again. Frustrated, he pulled back from following Jesus' boat. Padding beside the water's edge, he moved back to the town to wait there for Jesus.

[*] *for event seen through human eyes – p. 219*

152

Later in the morning he found the town almost deserted. There were a few elderly humans sweeping in front of their nests and watching young humans at play and some humans with carts full of food for sale, but most of the humans who lived in the town had gone. Solamen went to the big water and drank, and for a while he watched the little animals climbing out of their holes and standing on the edges. He caught one and ate it though its fellows chattered their anger at him. He waited a long time. Toward evening the humans started returning. They were quiet, subdued. Was it because Jesus had left them? They acted like field animals when they were left alone for a while by a lazy human leader.

It was days before Jesus returned. Solamen ran many miles each night searching the countryside, but though he could find traces left by his leader, he always arrived too late. Jesus had gone to another place.

By this time Solamen no longer worried about what he would eat. He preferred the tall birds that fished in the water, but they were hard to sneak up on. Always there were the little animals that played hide and seek. If he waited long enough, one would slip out of his hole into Solamen's paws. He would hold it between his paws as he severed its backbone with a good hard bite. High up in the mountains, though he hesitated to go so far from town because he might miss Jesus' return, were the swift little horned animals that jumped from rock to rock. It was a hit or miss game to catch one. Once, when he was but inches away from a plump little female, his toenails scraped trails of moss as he slipped from the rock she bounded from, and he fell the height of a man onto a rocky ledge. That day he had limped back to town and eaten the little players instead.

Finally, after many days of lying in wait, of losing weight and feeling a sadness in his very bones, one morning he heard the crowd coming from far away and shouting. It was shouting: "Jesus!" And Jesus came into town, his skin looking darker and sun-blessed, his hair longer and the animal strips covering his feet in tatters. It was then that the pack members discovered Solamen. And here is how it happened:

One of the female humans brought a male human up to Jesus. When Jesus questioned him, he shook his head and pointed to his ears. Then Jesus gave the back signal to all but three of his pack members, and with the male human, his mother, and those three he retreated back the way he had just come and off the path.

Solamen followed on the hill above them. He was so eager to touch Jesus that he was careless about remaining hidden. In fact, he wanted so badly to come to Jesus that holding his hindquarters high in the air, he pushed his face and neck into a Jesus' footprint and openly wiggled in frustration. Afterwards, still unsatisfied, he scratched the spot stiffly with both front paws, and in so doing sent a spray of dust and tiny stones arcing above him. The little follower saw him. His eyes grew round with astonishment. He picked up a rock and hurled it at Solamen. It fell short as Solamen immediately retreated deep into the bushes. Jesus simply observed the play. Then he looked to the deaf man.

Into the deaf ears Jesus put his fingers, one on each side of the man's head so that they looked like ear extensions, or maybe like the kind of double view of everything Solamen saw after he was hit on the head by the boat. Solamen picked up his own ears as he saw Jesus spit and then with one hand pull down the man's jaw and with the other, place the spittle upon his tongue. Immediately the man began dancing and screaming like the one who was lowered through the roof. Jesus put out his hand to quiet him, but the man only ran around faster yelling Jesus' name. Then he ran off toward the crowds. The man's mother, her body bowed in apology, moved close to Jesus. And he comforted her, patting her arm and walking with her back to the crowds.[*]

It was very late that night that Jesus settled down with his pack in the nest in which he usually slept. All the other followers had left and as Solamen dozed behind the bushes, the door to the nest cracked open and a stream of light came forth, waking Solamen. The light was partially blocked by a tall figure, his leader. Jesus called softly: "Solamen."

Startled, Solamen moved forward to a place he had never before been invited. His whole body slinked as a vandal's did as it cruised through the forest. His tail hung low and his breath came short and swift.

Soon he was at the threshold, then inside. He stood trembling. But those inside, sitting cross-legged on the floor with crusts of bread sopping up the last bits of juice from a pot, drew back. They too were startled. Like the conquered people when the Romans broke down doors. One of them jumped up, picked up a small, hard drinking cup and raised it to throw. But Jesus gave him the "down" signal and he sat. Solamen thought Jesus' signal was meant for him and he settled stiffly at his pack leader's feet.

[*] *for event seen through human eyes – p. 219*

155

Jesus turned to face his pack: "I want you all to know about this dog," he said. "Today Andrew saw him following me. Andrew threw a stone at him because he thinks him unclean.

"So I have brought him into this place tonight to tell you he is not unclean. Nothing that goes into a man is unclean, but only that which comes out. Have I not touched the lepers, and the women with issues of blood? Have I not sent you out to do the same? Then why do you worry about this one and his uncleanliness? And not the others named in the proscriptions? Did not my Father on the sixth day create all kinds of living creatures: cattle, creeping things and wild animals, and did he not see how good it was? Not how unclean?

"This dog that you see here tonight protected my cousin John from a large cat. John did not name him, but I have. His name is Solamen." At the sound of his name Solamen's ears flicked forward; his breath slowed, and he turned his head from watching the pack to gazing at Jesus. His eye became limpid, adoring golden pools.

"Andrew knows that although John would not allow this dog into his cave, he fed him at times and enjoyed his protection as he kept away many who would hurt John. He has come to me now. Some could take an example from him because he asks nothing, not even food and shelter. Yet he loves me. And nothing gets in the way of his love for me. He would willingly give his life for me and does not expect a special place in my kingdom. Instead, he is one of the many good things given me by my Father. When I am exhausted from the press of the crowds, when I have given and given of the power within until I am almost depleted, I go to the mountain to pray and renew myself. He joins me and brings his warm furry body for comfort. He loves simply sitting beside me. Touching and being touched. He does not question me nor make demands. He believes that he is protecting me because that is one of the jobs that creatures such as he is, do. You who are my closest friends, know that I need no protection. I have told you that no one can take my life from me, that I must lay it down myself. But he would not understand that. Thus, although you are wrong in believing him unclean, you may be sure there will be no mention of him in salvation history. He will never take your place in my heart.

"Now you are probably asking: 'If this is so, why do you hide him from your followers?' And I answer you that right now my people are hearing so many messages, it will be easier if they do not yet hear this one. It will come in due time.

"Before you jump to any conclusions about what others should be able to handle, remember when you were out in the boat during a storm? I was right there with you. You remember being frightened? You trembled and called out in fear. You are with me day after day. I speak plainly to you, my close friends, and not in parables,. You should know that I would not let you be harmed. Yet when the storm descended, you remembered not my words. So if even you cannot believe all that I tell you, can you expect it of the others? With whom I share only in parables? If any of my people discovers this one that I call Solamen, I will explain him. But if he hides and only shares his warmth with me when I am away from the crowds, that is good. You know that John asked the people to take a large step into righteousness, to repent. I am now asking them to go so much further: to love, not only the Lord their

157

God, and their neighbors, but their enemies as well. This is an overwhelming task. Right now I do not want to scandalize and confuse them with additional truths and changes.

"Gradually they will learn all that I am teaching you. But for now I am telling you, do not seek to ignore all the traditions of my people, but neither allow them to get in the way of my message. As for this animal, I do not expect you to like or touch him, but do ask you with me to thank my Father for him as one of his good things given."

Solamen then heard Jesus call Andrew, the one who had tried to stone Solamen, up to the front of the room. Jesus motioned Solamen up to the "sit" position as Andrew drew near. Then he motioned for Andrew's large, suntanned hand to touch Solamen. Reluctant, but obedient, Andrew touched Solamen with a light quick touch on his head that made both of them shiver. A few others came forth hesitatingly and lightly touched as if fearing Solamen would snap. Finally Solamen saw the youngest approach, slowly and inquisitively. He extended his hand sideways and instead of the short light touch on the head, he placed his hand on Solamen's side where Jesus had cured him. Solamen felt the warmth of his touch and sensed that he had wanted to pat Solamen for a long time. In fact, Solamen felt that even beyond his inquisitiveness, this one would have hugged Solamen if invited by his pack leader. But Jesus seemed more intent on the next follower. Jesus' mother, leaving her task of cleaning the pot which had held supper, advanced gracefully. At her approach Solamen whined uneasily and stood on all four strong legs. Just a few inches from him she laughed softly and withdrew her outstretched hand – not, he could feel, in fear, but in acknowledgement of his reluctant feelings.

Solamen was confused. In a small area next to Jesus he shifted his weight from one stiff leg to another. Never had a woman been unafraid of him. Never had a woman emitted signals like hers. Like Solamen, like Jesus, she felt more than what could be seen. She felt. She knew the inside feelings of Solamen and respected them. What about the pack? Did she understand each of them as he did? Did she feel the disquiet of the tight-skinned one who was always counting the metal pieces? Did she feel the exuberant happiness of the youngest one who wanted to hug him? What about the confusion of the one who had thrown the rock at him and then, at Jesus' word, touched him?

After as many as would, touched Solamen, Jesus knelt on one knee and hugged him to himself. At that Solamen relaxed his whole body and leaned into Jesus, whining and slurping his large wet nose and tongue on Jesus' cheek. Jesus laughed and released him. He put his strong shoulder to the door, opened it and motioned him out.

Solamen walked stiffly out. His legs felt as if they had been asleep a long time. After the door closed behind him Solamen sniffed it to his heart's content. He sniffed the length of the threshold, then up and down the seam of the door. He stood on his hind feet, whining softly and struggling to smell every scent that escaped through the crack in the door. As he pulled the scents seeping from the inside over the fine hairs which lined his nostrils, he quivered. Finally he had his fill. His body relaxed and he trotted off to sleep.

CHAPTER XVI

Release

Each time that Jesus and his pack got into the boats, Solamen whined and fretted. He knew that it would be a long time until he saw Jesus again. Each time that Jesus returned, and when Solamen had a chance to get close to him, Solamen could smell on his foot coverings all the places Jesus had been: the places with lush greens, the places below mountains, and the places on a large body of water which was salty and undrinkable, unlike the water near Jesus' borrowed nest.

Each time that Jesus left and the crowds had dwindled and then left, Solamen would go down to the shoreline and smell his leader's footprints. Sometimes he would want to advance into the water. But the memory of the storm and the boat which crashed into his head terrified him. It kept him from following Jesus.

One day Jesus came as usual to the sea shore to meet and speak to a particularly large crowd. He had come by boat, and it was anchored off shore. All morning Solamen watched Jesus from where he lay hidden as Jesus greeted the humans, held their young ones, and touched their sick. Any who wanted could come close to Jesus. Except for Solamen. He had not been able to get close to Jesus for so many days that his stomach hurt and his shoulders as well. He chewed his feet in frustration. He knew that Jesus' boat would leave as soon as he finished talking, and he would have another day without Jesus. It was unbearable. He wanted to run down through the crowd to Jesus, but he knew the commotion he would cause. The humans would scream and yell and throw things at him; (he didn't care if they did), but much worse, Jesus would give him the "back" signal. He hated that more than a Roman whipping! So he stayed hidden and watched.

Finally, he saw some of Jesus' pack members get into one of the boats. Jesus was giving his farewell sign from the middle of the crowd which was already thinning. His remaining pack members were still speaking with some of the other humans. Then, off to the side a roar went up as a little female human, who arrived on a flat, carrying piece, jumped and ran from Jesus into her mother's arms. Everyone in the crowd, including the remaining pack members, rushed to see her. Jesus went the opposite direction into the boat.

Jesus' boat started off, while the second boat waited for the remaining pack members. This time Jesus' boat did not go far out but stayed close to the shoreline. Solamen was determined to follow. He struggled through the underbrush, getting covered with the sticky little plant pieces that attached to his fur, but he kept going until the land ended in a drop-off. To continue on land he would have had to work his way from the water's edge and around a bend to a place from which he could not see the boat. He stopped and whined, then jumped angrily into the water, desperate to reach a piece of land jutting out a short distance across. But when he splashed into the water, he realized that his feet did not touch bottom, and he panicked. Struggling frantically, he bobbed up and down and swallowed large amounts of water. Then suddenly, he felt warmth from the Jesus' boat. It touched his chest and wandered through his shoulders up into his head and down through his legs filling him and calming him. He saw Jesus with his raised arm watching him. Surprisingly, he began to swim easily, bringing round his legs until they almost touched, bobbing his shoulders in and out of the water until, his head held high, he swam through the water swirling around his neck. Thus, at last, he gave up his fear of the water to follow Jesus.

"Hurrah! Hurrah!" came the rousing shout from Jesus' boat. It had stopped in the water. The pack members were using their sturdy tree paddles to hold back the speed of the floating nest. And the pack members were shouting him on. That felt good.

When the pack resumed paddling both nests with Solamen swimming beside the Jesus' one, they did not pull forward as hard as usual. Both nests slowed to allow him to keep up. As he swam he began to enjoy the coolness of the water on his skin. He felt the sun as well, and the little breezes. And as he passed trees and bushes and beaches, he smelled the different animals that lived in those places. So this time he didn't lose Jesus. He knew where Jesus was when he left by way of the water, and today they arrived at the base of a mountain together. Solamen shook himself as he emerged onto firm ground, sending droplets of gleaming water in a large circle over the earth. This time the pack would wait below for Jesus' return while Solamen and Jesus climbed to the top of the mountain. Solamen felt a delicious thrill as he planned to rest his head in Jesus' lap. With his tongue lolling out, happily he waited for Jesus to call him apart.

But that is not what happened.

Peter, who always reacted swiftly like a goaded beast in the amphitheater; the young one, John; and John's brother, James; climbed out of the nest and pulled it onto the sand. Up the mountain they went after Jesus. They were strong, like Solamen, leading an outdoor life. They pulled in large nets full of water animals far into each night. But they had trouble keeping up with Jesus. He was on a mission this day and he moved swiftly to the top of the mountain as if he was expecting to meet someone or something. Solamen could feel his anticipation, and he wove himself around the other three, brushing their legs as he marched up beyond them, until he was right behind Jesus.

Something – not anything challenging – but something in the way that Jesus stood on top of the mountain astounded him. It may have been the tautness of his muscles, or the way that he pulled himself to a height not shown before, not even when he reprimanded the ones who wore the dangling metal pieces. But even after that long, hard climb up the mountain, Jesus stood mightier than any animal that, with every hair standing on end, would draw itself to its full height. His posture would have made any animal within a feeling radius, tingle, flail and submit. And Solamen did submit, collapsing to the ground and whining. He was ready for whatever was coming. And then it came:

Behind Jesus the fog rose. Yet here, the light, more radiant than that which rises on a clear day, painted his face, his beard and his covering so that Solamen squinted at his brightness and that of two strangers who now appeared beside him. The wind blew the little branches on the ground into circles. And with all the power of the skies it blew a path through the tall thistles until they bowed and touched the ground before Jesus. And the pack members? It reached them too, and knocked them to the ground where they lay supine, trembling, close to whimpering.

Why hadn't they, like Solamen, known earlier that something unusual was happening with Jesus? Instead they had come from their climb unaware, chatting happily and drinking from the animal pockets that held water . . . until they had been felled like trees in a storm. Today they had been the dumb ones. He may be a dumb dog. He had been called that by Taursus. But today he was the first to feel this coming.

Now he gloried fully in the power of Jesus. He could see and feel the power reach his inmost being. He had always felt something inner about Jesus. Today it struck him to his core.

When the brightness ceased, the other two, on either side of Jesus, left, and Jesus stood looking quietly at his pack. Solamen was the first to move. He rolled happily over on his back, rubbing his large neck on the bumpy soil, then the bone at the top of his shoulders, then down his spine until he was wiggling his hips and slinging his large tail back and forth to sweep the broken thistles from the path.

Having felt Jesus' overwhelming power he now knew something more about Jesus. He was truly the strongest leader. No one was strong enough to kill him. No one. Not even Ursus. Or the Roman soldiers.[*]

---

[*] *for event seen through human eyes – p. 219*

165

As Solamen rolled quickly back up onto his feet, he knew suddenly with certainty that he had never protected Jesus. When he went with him to the mountain, he was not protecting Jesus from the vandals and thieves as he had protected John. Jesus could protect himself. So the only reason Jesus could want Solamen on the mountain with him was simply because he loved him. All that he could give Jesus was comfort and warmth.

Solamen watched the pack members rise and stumble anxiously over to Jesus. They spoke over each other. They made breathless appeals, the way an animal would that was jumping and begging for a piece of meat. Jesus only shook his head, and with a pat on the head for Solamen and a gesture with his arm to them, he started down the mountain. Solamen could tell that whatever they had offered Jesus, it was not something he wanted. And Solamen knew that they, like himself, had some wrong ideas about Jesus. Why could they not simply tuck in their tails, scrunch up to Jesus, lie still and feel his love?

Solamen, the least of the pack members, trailed the others happily. When they were almost to the base of the mountain, Solamen heard the noise of a great crowd. Some voices were strident with anger, snapping and growling, vandals after a kill. Others were expectant, those who knew and were waiting for a feast. There were very many. It seemed that at every stop Jesus made, more and more humans waited for him. Many tried to touch him. Some actually reached for his sleeves and tried to stop him. Some blocked his way and his pack members had to push them gently to the side to form a path for Jesus. Jesus usually found a small hill to stand on so that the gathered humans could see him. And usually, when he got up on that hill (one time he mounted a cart with vegetables;

sometimes he went into a boat close to shore), the crowd quieted and those in the back stopped pushing. It seemed that Jesus wanted to help them all and the cheers that went up when he touched and cured a sick one were as robust as the cheers in the amphitheater after a kill.

Today, at the sight of the first covered head below, Solamen stopped and slinked back up the hill to a place from which he could watch without being seen. As he gazed down at the crowd, someone came to the front to question Jesus. Questions again. Always questions. Jesus could have ignored them or chased them away as any pack leader could do. But he always answered.

Today, this questioner was a human father coming through a parting crowd with a grown male son who was grinding his teeth. Jesus touched the son and he fell to the ground, thrashing and foaming at the mouth. Solamen had seen a bitch do that in her cage under the amphitheater. And the soldiers had opened the cage and pulled her out without even wearing hand covering. When they extracted her, they speared her and she put up no defense, but lay, as this human did, twitching her limbs and foaming at the mouth until the blood gurgled forth from her throat at her death.

Within moments the human son lay still like a dead one. But with the wind coming toward Solamen, he knew from its wafting smells there was no dying here. Instead, the son jumped to his feet, then danced and ran circles around Jesus, then fell on his knees and kissed Jesus' hand over and over. Solamen felt a pang that it was not he licking that hand. In his sitting spot he whined and moved his hips impatiently.*

* *for event seen through human eyes – p. 219*

Now that Solamen wholeheartedly embraced a leader it was harder and harder for him to lie at a distance from him. Jesus let all the others come to him. The male humans, the female humans, the limping ones and those led by others. Jesus touched them and fed them until his large pack grew to a truly unmanageable size. But another pack was also forming, one seeking to down Jesus and take over the lead. In it were the ones with their metal fringes who came and argued with him. They ate the food he gave to the crowd. But at the same time they seemed not to notice the cures he worked. They argued with red faces, or drew from their pockets dried plant pieces from which they read questions. They shouted and interrupted Jesus when he addressed the crowds.

Each day it got harder for Jesus to talk with those who came in earnest. Harder to heal those who needed his touch. Often, just as Jesus was getting into a boat, or turning to walk away, someone else would break through the crowd and come rushing up with a sick human, and, though Jesus' sagging posture showed Solamen that he was exhausted, he would stop. The power inside Jesus would touch that person. Solamen always felt it reverberate, swelling his own body, filling it until it reached its boundaries and beyond to dizzy him. He found it thrilling. But at the same time he disliked it because he felt out of control of his muscles and head. So Solamen tried to avoid the experience. He tried to move far away, but his limbs refused. He was immobilized by his loyalty with Jesus. So he sat and endured, watching the sick one recover and feeling the ebb-and-flow echo of that amazing energy within his own body. It dissipated so slowly and left him tired. No wonder that giving that healing touch over and over would tire Jesus as well. Yet, though Jesus' steps slowed and he took leave of his followers, he often would stop for another. Even halfway into the boat with his robe lifted and hand on the wooden side, he would turn back to touch another needy human. All these strangers rushed toward Jesus, famine-starved as mice. They received his touch, yet Solamen could not go to him. He so much wanted to.

Jesus moved around the big water to a new place each day. Each night he was in a different nest. Once he and his close pack slept in the boats. A few times he returned to the nest in which he had introduced Solamen to his close pack members. But Solamen was never invited back inside. When Solamen did get to approach Jesus, it was for a very short time and not often. No matter how late, the areas close to the nests were seldom vacant. Solamen even had to change bushes a few times to avoid the humans coming off the path to get to a nest. Late at night they trampled plants and occasionally knocked over water pots and stumbled and fell down steps. Solamen slept with one eye open for them as if keeping watch for vandals. A few times he scared one away who came unexpectedly upon him, but usually he heard someone coming, and moved away.

One night it rained. It rained hard. Thunder and lightning made Solamen seek shelter below the place he usually slept. It lit the faces of those who waited outside the nest where Jesus was staying. The wind howled and the rain pounded so hard that they all fled – almost as on a signal. Toward morning the sky quieted. Jesus came out with all his pack. They carried their branches and some animal skins with water. They walked out of town on the wet road leading toward the big water. Solamen trotted through puddles on that road to get to Jesus. Reaching him from behind, he touched Jesus' ankle with his wet nose, and Jesus turned around and hugged him. He took Solamen's large head into his hands, forming them around his neck where the spiked metal collar once had lain. But unlike that collar, Jesus' encircling left him free to pull away if he wanted. Of course he didn't.

As Jesus strode up the road from the nesting place, he gave Solamen the "back" signal. Soon many began joining Jesus, coming from different nesting places, sitting by the side of the road waiting to go. Others came with gifts of fruit and dried grain for him, pieces of dried field animal and large skins of water. Jesus' mother met them as well. And Solamen, impatient at the speed of the traveling group, thought following the group as slow as following a desert animal which lumbered down the road from one side to the other under its large shell.

Nonetheless, Solamen stayed behind, out of sight. He did run and chase the small animals and had himself feasts. He even took small naps before running to catch up. It was obvious to him that Jesus was not going back to his last nesting place. He began to have memories because of the direction the group was taking. The earth was lush in places that were usually dry. Rain came often and drew the plants upright and made them flower. The little birds would attack them greedily, not noticing the large black dog waiting motionless for his own supper.

As he followed, he knew that the road was descending down through an area even more lush than that through which they had come. This area was always lush. It had growing plants different from those of the road behind. Flowers were everywhere and the humans there had made their nests bigger than those they had left. Still they had humans unable to walk. One sat by the roadside holding a pan out to those who passed. Jesus touched him and he gave up his roadside post. Solamen watched the crowd from a higher vantage point, and he saw the crowd surround the man and then pull back again like the big salty water playing with the beach. They all walked on.

CHAPTER XVII

Betrayal

They had walked for days. They had slept together under the stars, or in nests in small towns. Then one morning after Solamen had scouted the area and come back to watching the stragglers of the crowd, they all began cheering. One ran to the edge of the road, and taking a large knife from under his covering, he cut handfuls of feathery looking greens. He handed them to the people around. Soon others did the same.

That day was a tough one for Solamen. He, who was now so obedient to Jesus, who had done his every bidding, who had remained out of sight, now saw Jesus rise above the crowd. They had lifted him above themselves before and Solamen was used to it. But here, today, Jesus was lifted onto another animal. This animal was going into the big city with Jesus. This animal would feel Jesus' legs gripping him, Jesus' hands on his neck, Jesus' every breath as he took in and expelled air, as he spoke to the crowds. And as he had so long ago with Taursus, Solamen would have to stay out, to stay behind. Solamen was not allowed in. Solamen lay with his face between his paws, his eyes cloudy with disappointment.

Again he lay outside the city gate.

Much, much later, long after the usual evening meal, Jesus came out. Without a glance toward Solamen he took his close pack members on the road, and, after a short walk entered a nesting place. The animal that Jesus rode was no longer with him. Had he disappointed Jesus? Had the humans not wanted him near? Was he too "unclean?"

This time only his close pack members followed Jesus to the nesting place. And Solamen trotted far behind, searching with nose and eye for a nesting place of his own.

It was still dark the next day when Jesus pushed open the door. Solamen ran quickly from his alert status behind some bushes to scrunch up and lean against him. He petted Solamen dutifully, but they did not connect. Because of the swift, light touch, Solamen knew that Jesus' heart was far away. Inside he was somewhere else. In fact, later that day Jesus became uncharacteristically angry, almost the way Taursus did after drinking the sour stuff. The pack was on the road with him when they came to a fruit tree. Jesus stepped close and looked up into it. His body, both lax and stressed, said "disappointment," as if one of the little round darting animals had evaded his dinner plan. Jesus struck the tree and yelled at it. None of his pack said anything. All stopped talking. Soon they resumed their walk to Jerusalem, and this time Jesus walked too. Maybe he was angry to have lost his mount. Once a soldier got a mount, he kept it unless it was killed in battle. Maybe the field animal Jesus rode the day before, had done a poor job. Or maybe it ran away because it did not want to be with Jesus. Solamen would have willingly carried Jesus until he collapsed.

Day after day Jesus went into the big city and stayed until dark. Then he came back and ate at the new nest. Solamen knew that his inner stuff was still far away. Jesus was uneasy about something, like a mother field animal that knows her young are being watched by predators. Solamen had smelled and felt that emotion on his hunts. He knew it well.

During these days the tight-skinned one often came back early from the city ahead of the others. He would go to the fruit carts and buy fruit, but Solamen sensed that his real mission was to meet there with one of the humans who wore the long pieces with the metal attached and who also bought fruit. They spoke vigorously together. Solamen saw that neither cared for the fruit they fingered. They only cared about the business they were doing together. When he watched them, he felt the same electricity that he had from his cage in the amphitheater as he watched the buying and selling of humans for the bloody games. As he walked away, the human who came to meet the tight-skinned one, would throw his fragrant, ripe globes into the weeds.

At night when the pack returned, the tight-skinned one would have fruit ready for the returning pack. He would first pick the ripest smelling for himself and then offer the remaining, first to Jesus, then the others. Whenever Jesus asked, he would dig into his clothing and pull out the nest of metal pieces and show him, but he never showed Jesus the cache of metal pieces he kept in the bulging nests imbedded in his leather belt around his stomach.

Solamen could tell that he didn't like distributing the metal pieces. His body warmed a bit when he fingered them, but it stiffened as he threw pieces to the humans who limped and babbled and cried to Jesus. He would deliberately throw a metal piece past an outstretched hand, and then watch the other human grovel on the ground to retrieve it.

When he joined the pack, he had been a better follower. He walked as if on springy grass. He hurried and pushed to be close to Jesus. Nonetheless, from the start, Solamen had sensed some confusion in him and had not trusted him. Solamen had been glad that on the night that Jesus had offered him to the pack to be touched, this tight-skinned one had pulled back. Solamen would have shuddered at his touch. How he wished that Jesus would send him away! Didn't Jesus tire of his constant arguments? How he didn't look at Jesus? Didn't he notice how this one's body always turned slightly away when he was talking to Jesus? His greetings, his embrace at meeting each day, was quick and hard, like being bumped by a tree. He didn't melt into the warmth which was Jesus, like the others, like Solamen. Didn't Jesus feel this one's resistance when he was near him? Perhaps Solamen was better as a rage-feeler than Jesus. He had had such rage himself. He remembered how long ago he himself had, filled with wickedness, lay in wait to torment the little field animals until they were lifeless.

With this tight-skinned one Solamen felt that there was a rival pack member among them, just waiting to take down Jesus. In his dreams Solamen would see the tight-skinned one throw his metal pieces at Jesus until they surrounded him and made a huge pile atop him. As he lay on his side, legs outstretched, Solamen would twitch and make sharp little half-bark sounds, and when he woke he did not feel as refreshed as usual.

Of course, there was nothing he could do to protect Jesus. But then he remembered. The branch. John's branch. He could get it and take it to Jesus. He could not protect Jesus, but he could bring him comfort. In his dreams he took the branch to Jesus and dropped it at his feet. The look in Jesus' eyes, as he gently picked it up, turned Solamen's own eyes to liquid love. His happy wagging tail thumped a rhythm on the ground which made the little night creatures scurry out of reach of the sleeping dog.

Toward evening of one day Jesus took his close pack to a large nest close to the big city. Perfume from the little flowers in the trees filled the air. Unlike the usual evening inactivity, this night humans bustled and made their noises as if it were the middle of the day. Some made late deliveries of baked and crushed field plants and casks of the sour drink Taursus loved. Solamen looked for a resting place, but none could be found. In fact, so many humans had screamed upon discovering him in a resting place outside a nest or even close to the road, that he decided to go elsewhere, to find a place where humans would not scream and hop back upon finding him.

He walked east away from the commotion, but the road was still crowded with many humans coming to the big city. Too busy here for him to sleep. He continued for hours until the crowd thinned to a mix of stragglers: those with lame or overburdened pack animals; old ones who walked slower than the rest; young ones delaying as much as possible the meeting with parents waiting outside the city gate. As he finally settled down into a gully off the road, he smelled fresh water. It wafted toward him on the strengthening breeze. Pulling the tiny droplets into his nostrils, he recognized it as the water that John had stood in. Flash backs to John illuminated his brain: John; his

177

speaking on the river; his pushing people down into the water; Jesus with John; Jesus walking away with his followers; John's climb up the hill; the death-defying cat fight; John's cave . . . John's branch. Now sleep was far from his goal. He was wide awake. He stood, shook himself and ran to the river. Like a pup seeking a lost toy he wanted that branch. He wanted to lie on it, run his breath over it and absorb any lingering smells. He wanted to get it and take it back to Jesus' temporary nest before morning. He had had a run-away like this under Taursus when he had disobeyed and left the city gate. Tonight he was on his own. He did not have to worry about being disobedient and leaving his post. He had no post. Yet he was uneasy. He was worried that something bad was going to happen to Jesus. He was worried that Jesus would not use his power to stop it. Yet he knew Jesus was not alone. He was with his close pack members. Surely they would keep him out of danger. Yet, as Solamen started forward again, he paused. He turned around and sat. He sat there for a while, under the full moon which threw its beams upon the river. Somehow he felt he was betraying Jesus by leaving, that now more than ever Jesus would want him close for comfort. But why?

He turned back to the branch and his longing to retrieve it. Jesus would be busy at the big nest for a long time. He might be out all night with his pack members, going to different nests, eating and talking. Solamen would get the branch and take it back to the temporary nest before Jesus got there. It would be there when Jesus returned. So Solamen left his post and galloped purposefully beside the river, continuing until he covered the distance to where John pushed people in. At the river, no longer afraid of Romans and storms, he plunged in. The water was cold and invigorating. Just as the night air, it carried a bit of a nip that energized him. When he reached the other side, he shook himself until the droplets gleamed in the waxing moon light. Then he trotted up the hillside to the cave.

As he approached he saw the large stone outcropping. Weeds grew where he used to sleep. They choked his passage. So he walked around to the front of the cave. There the weeds had been matted down into a well-traveled path. There his skin started to tingle as the smell of vandals pulled sharply over his fine nostril hairs and invaded his head and throat. Were they here right now? Once he had chased them far away. He crouched low and crawled slowly to the entrance of the cave. He crawled through plots of dried urine and feces and he could distinguish the smells of many: females and males and the young. All had been here. In fact, from the strength of the smells he knew they now lived here. In John's cave. A vandal nest in John's cave! Anger boiled up in him and without a thought for caution, he burst into the cave.

It was empty. But as the cool evening air surrounded his neck and shoulders, his feet felt the warmth of the bodies which had very recently lain on the ground. Obviously they were out hunting.

He was angry that these wretched creatures used John's cave. He had never been allowed in. Yet now they defiled it. Even he knew these were unclean. He walked around stiff-legged and angry, inspecting every bit of ground and high up on every wall, even way back in the cave where it was cold already though the night air had not reached it. He stood on his hind legs and stretched. Then, slowly backing down, he sniffed the ground. Bat dung stung his nose. He almost missed it . . .

The branch. Lying as far back in the cave as possible, half wedged under a damp, descending rock, and covered with droplets of bat dung, was where he found it. He used his paws on it. He scraped away the dung. He sneezed and his mouth leaked spittle as he worked. Twice he moved away, miserable. No matter how hard he tried he could not dislodge it. Then he knew that he had to do it. He had to grab it with his mouth. No matter how distasteful. And he did. He grabbed it hard with his mouth, trying not to fully connect his tongue and jowls to the dung-stained branch, trying to leave room for air. He worked his paws, claws extended, in unison with his pulling mouth. No success.

Then they came. The vandals. He heard them outside the cave. Just two voices. They did not rush in. They were smarter than that. Besides, they were cowards. They obviously smelled him. They were waiting for back up. They became very silent. But he could hear their breathing, and he knew they could hear his. He could run through them. Take them by surprise. And probably get away before the rest of their pack arrived. But without the branch?

He went back to work. Cautiously. In fits and starts because he was alert now to the breathing sounds. Were they closer? Were there more? After each pull at the branch he stopped to listen. And finally he heard a third vandal's rhythmic breath. Behind him this one stepped slowly into the cave. His breathing got louder.

Solamen clamped down without caution on the disgusting branch; pieces of dung, clinging to the branch were released into his throat. He stiffened his legs, and pulled so hard that he dislodged the branch in a spray of dirt, dung and little stones that sent him with the branch many feet from the wall, flat on his back with his feet flailing. A chance for the vandals to rush in. Solamen down and vulnerable. But instead he heard the ambitious one retreat from the cave. Perhaps, like the little animals which ran from him during his happy dreams, she thought Solamen was stronger, or bigger, or instead of an accidental fall, that scraping on the cave floor had been orchestrated by Solamen on purpose. One thing about the vandals: they were more cunning than the fighter dogs of the amphitheater. They did not waste their lives on unproductive fights.

Solamen walked stiffly to the cave entrance, carrying the branch in his mouth. In the moonlight outside he could see more vandals coming from all sides, many more. Like the humans who came to Jesus they were female, male, and young. Unlike most of Jesus' followers, they were coming to destroy.

When the second vandal crossed the line into the cave, Solamen dropped the branch and walked stiffly toward her. Solamen's hair was standing on end. His ears were tight against his head. His tail shifted slow and low from side to side. His eyes flashed with green glints. A deep guttural sound came from deep within and it did not stop. The vandal swirled swiftly on her front toes, and leaving the cave, came to a sit-stop a few feet out.

It was a come-on. A ploy. Solamen did not fall for it. He sensed that if he chased the vandal into the open it would give the others a way into the cave behind him. He would be surrounded. His only hope was that none would be brave enough to attack within the cave.

He was right about that. None was willing to attack the monster animal with the huge head and the growl that went on all night like an approaching storm. Toward morning the vandals moved restlessly. A few left and Solamen sensed they were off for a hunt, leaving others to guard at the nest lest he try to leave. As the light of the moon waned, Solamen heard the sounds of the hunt up in the hills. He could tell from their shrieks and laughs that the vandals were chasing a large animal; the other vandals knew it too. And by this time, as they left one by one to join the hunt, only a few males with their offspring remained. They moved around unhappily, listening to the triumphant loud cackles that told them the animal had been brought down. It was ready to be feasted on. And so, looking guilty, one by one they left their post.

As soon as the last little one followed the others up the hill behind the cave, Solamen grabbed the branch. He shook it mightily to dislodge the remaining dung and ran down the hill. It was morning now. Nothing was in his way. The sounds of the vandals got fainter and fainter. He knew they could never trace him through the water he would swim.

But carrying the branch was no easy task. As he descended, jumping a boulder, one side of the branch slanted downward until it dug into the ground, jarring him and throwing him over.

His jaws ached as he rose and gingerly took the branch back into his mouth. He held it near the end that had dug the hole; but pretty soon he was down again, this time the other end digging into the soil. He sat up. He ran his tongue over a smattering of blood on his tongue. He coughed. He looked quizzically at his prize. He pounded it with both front paws. But it never moved. It never fought back.

So finally, he took one end of the branch into his mouth and cautiously pulled it through the dirt and small bushes. That worked. But it was hard. It was slow. He had to bend his legs, crouch and walk backwards down the hill.

As he moved downward he had no more trouble from the boisterous branch. So to speed things up he once again put his mouth on the center of the branch, lifted it and started walking forward. It was easy. He was making good time, but he decided to go faster and so began running . . . Again he got whacked. This time as he rose from the ground, he remembered. Jesus. His excursion was taking so much more time than he had planned. What about Jesus? Was he back already? Had he slept? The whole night had passed while he was in the cave surrounded by vandals, and where was Jesus? Jesus was probably headed back toward the city. Again he began to sense that all was not well with Jesus. That Jesus had not slept well either. That he had not made it back to the nesting place. Maybe he should leave the branch and search for Jesus.

But he had only a short way to go. And Jesus would be happy to have John's branch. And so he kept it. He came to the water with the branch between his teeth. He had alternated between carrying and dragging it. One tooth had been broken off in the process and blood dripped from his mouth.

As he approached the water, darkness came over the sky. The wind whipped the few weeds on the bank, and large drops of rain fell. Solamen whined. The wind grabbed the branch and jerked it from his mouth, knocking Solamen again to the ground. Once on the ground he saw the branch was being spun by the wind. So he half-crawled and half-jumped to retrieve it. He held it with his back feet while with his front paws, he dug a slight depression in the sand to hold it. To keep it there he spread the full length of his body upon it. When he did that, it was strange, for just as he had seemed so much larger than he was when confronting the vandals, now, on this branch, he seemed so much less.

With his legs outstretched and his tail tucked under, he suffered the pounding rain and howling wind . . . until once again his body signaled that someone important to him had died. Again he lost control over his insides. His urine ran from his body onto the beach. And his feces left his body in blobs until it liquefied and emptied him completely. That is how he knew that Jesus had died. His body ached, and he cried as he lay there on the beach. He cried because he so much loved Jesus. And now Jesus was gone. When all the others had called him "unclean" and been afraid to have him near, Jesus had loved him. Jesus had held him close on the trips to the mountain. Sometimes he had fed him and met him at night. He had cured him in John's cave and taught him to swim unafraid. How he loved Jesus! And how Jesus loved him! He would stay here on the shore, lying with this branch. He did not care if the sun parched him; he did not want to move ever again.

CHAPTER XVIII

Resurrection

He did not eat for thirty-six hours, through night, day and night. He lay outstretched on the river bank, feeling the bare branch tight against the side of his belly and in the crook of his front leg. Bereft and despairing. Until the sky lightened on the third day.

The light did not stay only in the sky. It came upon him. His body filled with energy. His chest began to tingle and like an army of ants the energy wended its way to his shoulders, his head, and down through his fore legs. It was as if Jesus had touched him. He whined. He sat and looked at the branch lying in the sand. Then quickly, he grabbed the branch and swam the now-calm river. On his way to the Jesus' nest he finally figured out how to handle the branch. He positioned it on one side of his large jowl, dragging it behind him so that it bounced a steady rhythm on the ground. There were sporadic, jarring bouts with protruding rocks which flipped it skyward, but those did not stop him. No more hole-digging to brake his advance and toss him into the dirt. He ran with long, easy strides. He ran on and on for hours, never stopping. He had a surplus of energy. He was as happy as he had been on the mountain with Jesus.

When he arrived at Jesus' nest late that morning, no one seemed to be home. It was a glorious day with a cool invigorating breeze. The trees were silver with the past rain and the bucket by the well half-filled with rain water, but there were no shoe coverings outside the door.

Solamen went up to the wooden door with the branch in his mouth to listen for voices inside. As he puzzled what to do, he turned at a noise coming toward him on the path. It was too late to hide as he always did, but he whirled anyway, looking for cover, and as he did the branch struck the door. And Jesus' mother came out at the knock. Smiling, she held her arms open in greeting, stunning Solamen. Until he realized the greeting was not for him, but for Jesus. Yes, Jesus was coming up the path. And he greeted and hugged his mother. Like a puppy she was so happy that she cried. Tears of joy ran down her face.

"I knew you would rise, my son," she finally blurted out. "Earlier the others took perfumed oils to your gravesite to anoint your body. I tried to dissuade them, to tell them you would not be there. You would rise as you said you would. But they love you too and they wanted to be sure you had the best. So I gave them my blessing and off they went . . . without me. I am so glad that I stayed."

"Mother," was all that Jesus said as he held her. Solamen saw a few tears in his eyes as well. It was as if the two of them were joined somehow, so close they were.

Solamen sat until Jesus acknowledged his presence and waved him into the nest. Every hair on his body stood straight as Jesus then hugged and patted him. Then Jesus went back out and brought in John's branch. He gave it to his mother and shortly after he was gone.

Solamen felt warm energy from Jesus' mother. He sensed that she knew things others did not, things no one told her, but things that came from the inside as they did with Jesus and John. She knew things others did not know about Jesus, even others close to him, like the young John and Andrew.

Solamen moved hesitatingly closer. Yes, this was a woman. A female human. This was the kind of human he had so despised. The kind of human he had most enjoyed scaring and whose soft flesh he had gloried in splitting. Now he knew he had been wrong to so despise one like this. A female human could be strong, stronger even than a male human. She could go her own way when all the others went another. He would never again despise female humans.

Jesus mother looked at the branch, clean now from its ride in the water. "John," she said softly as she fingered its length. Then she turned to Solamen: "You have brought his staff, Solamen. And I thank you."

Hearing his name Solamen moved closer, and finally, no longer able to hold back his happiness, he snuggled his large head under her hand pushing it up for attention. And she responded. "Solamen, Solamen," she purred as she patted his head, looking into his large liquid eyes. Then he felt her strong arms wrapping his heavy shoulders, her hand moving slowly over his back from his tail to his head, shoving the short hairs against the grain so that they stood like the thistles on the mountain. He shook them all flat again. She laughed at that and sat down among some pillows, pulling him with her until they both snuggled together in an embrace. He felt her fingers massage his paws, each toe and nail and in between. Finally as he lay with one of her legs partly under him he felt her hands starting under his eyes with firm strokes to his cheeks and under his jowls until he sighed with happiness, tumbled off her leg and lay flat upon his back.

She made them both a breakfast of grain. His was put into a large bowl, and on top she broke a few large raw eggs. They ate together on the floor, she sitting cross-legged; he standing over his bowl, savoring the contents. Then she escorted him back out.

Solamen came the following morning to Jesus' old meeting place. His mother was there, and very early she came out, as Jesus had done, and welcomed Solamen with a baked flying animal. John, Jesus' youngest pack member came that morning too, and the day after. He would stop on the way into the nest and whistle for Solamen. Then he petted him. Solamen liked John. He liked the way he gathered his ears into his hands and rubbed them between his fingers. He was never too gentle which would have made Solamen shake to get away, nor too strong, which would speak of dominance. He was instead, warm with a relaxed I-like-you kind of rub. John greeted Jesus' mother with the same I-like-you kind of kiss. They talked together as if they had not seen each other for many, many seasons; so much they had to say. They spoke Jesus' name often and seemed to surprise each other with what they said of him. Sometimes they would turn toward Solamen and speak his name. But they didn't call him to them. They did seem a bit troubled and their happy time would turn subdued as if they were concerned about his being there. Solamen was uneasy at those times. Should he leave and go into the hills? He couldn't do that. He was protecting Jesus' mother. Besides, it was certain that if he stayed near Jesus' mother, Jesus would come back to her and he would see Jesus again. All animals and humans repeat their actions. They return to the same places. They revisit their territories. Jesus would come back to his mother.

Occasionally Solamen would spend the night inside the nest. The pack members who nested with Jesus' mother became accustomed to his presence. Mostly female members, they knew he would protect them. If someone unknown to him as a pack member came to the door, he would slink into another room off the main path and lie with his ears toward the entrance.

One night late, all the members of the household had retired for the night. Jesus' mother had been sleeping on her mat, Solamen lying at her feet, when there came a knock at the door. That jerked him awake and he set himself between her and the doorway. She rose barefooted, gave him the "stay" signal, and pushing down on his shoulder with both hands, she squirmed around him and out the door. Solamen heard her pad through the hallway and on to the main door. After a brief whispering which Solamen could barely hear from his distance, he heard her open the door . . . to a Roman soldier. Solamen recognized the smell. He stood alert, his legs stiff, ears back and tail swinging slowly. He was ready to protect her.

But soon, from her unguarded tone, he knew she was welcoming someone she knew. From Solamen's experience he knew this person was a leader of soldiers. She called him "Centurion." There was a moment of silence and Solamen felt the warmth of touching between them. They spoke for a while, voices soft to keep the others in the nest from waking. Then Solamen heard her

189

moving near the fireplace and he heard the tinkle of a pot. She was making a hot drink for the soldier. Soon a soft squish of air released from a cushion announced his sitting down.

Jesus' mother left the room and Solamen heard her walk past his doorway and through the nest to another door. John, the youngest pack member, had slept there. Last night he had come late and stayed as he sometimes did. He would leave in the morning. Two pair of footsteps walked out from his doorway and into the large center room. Solamen heard a cup rattle as it was placed down onto the stone floor. Next he heard back slaps and hearty welcomes. John and the Roman to each other. Now he knew that this was one of the few Romans who followed Jesus. Not a close pack member, but a follower nonetheless. He recognized the short military stops in his speech. Was he looking here for Jesus? Apparently not. He was not speaking Jesus' name. He was obviously not sharing a "sighting" as so many did these days. In fact, he was speaking Solamen's name over and over. What he came for had to do with Solamen, not Jesus. For Solamen that was both puzzling and disturbing.

Solamen listened from his place behind the door. The Centurion was trying to persuade Jesus' mother to do something concerning Solamen. He kept asking the same question, over and over, but she did not agree. Finally, John, who had been quiet and had sat listening to the Centurion and Jesus' mother, spoke. He spoke to Jesus' mother and sadness was in his voice. How could he be sad when Jesus had just come back to them? The sadness revolved around his name, "Solamen." When John said it, Solamen could hear the breathless intonation and knew that John's throat muscles were slightly contracting. He thought of a field animal leaving her young for another nest.

Jesus' mother gave a deep sigh. It was the only time since Jesus had come to visit her that Solamen had heard her any way but happy.

Then he heard footsteps coming his way. John pulled back the door and motioned for Solamen to come out and into the room. He held his hand on Solamen's head and Solamen could feel his stress, straight down to his toes. He whimpered.

"Here he is!" he said to the Centurion. "Please promise me that you will be good to him. He is getting old and running beside your horse for a long way may be too difficult."

"You will not regret this decision," the Centurion answered. "I will always remember how Jesus loved him and will make sure he gets the best food and a loving home. Unlike your people, my people love dogs. They don't see them as "unclean." They let them live with them.

"Besides, no way will he be safe here. As I have told you both, the high priests and others are angry. They hated your son. In their searing hate they are looking for someone to punish. If they see you with a Roman army dog, they will say that you stole it. They will hold you captive. They will whip you and maybe cripple you. And they will take the dog away with them anyway. Neither the dog nor you will benefit. All Jesus' followers will likely be marked as thieves."

At that he stooped, and taking an animal strip from his skin bag, he walked over to Solamen. He tried to circle Solamen's head. Solamen ducked, but John caught him around his chest as he headed back to the sleeping room. Solamen felt John's strong young body hold against his pushing. Solamen could have easily pushed John aside, but he had come to respect John. He would not harm him, nor even push him away.

"Give me the collar," John said, and the Centurion dropped it into his hand. Solamen whined as he felt the leather sink down and encircle his neck. It was a bit tight. But then, he hadn't worn a collar in a long time. John took a rope from a hook beside the door and attached it to the collar. He handed the rope to the Centurion. Solamen rose on his back feet like a war animal as the Centurion pulled him firmly toward the door. Solamen spun back toward the hallway, but the Centurion held fast, one foot on the rope, the other looped through the door post. And Solamen dropped back down on all four feet his strong neck still pulling backwards.

John gave Solamen the "stay" signal, hand extended, fingers apart. Solamen began trembling. He was aware that Jesus' mother was trembling too. She came over to him, and as Solamen looked into her eyes, he felt that he was looking into her and seeing Jesus. He wanted to stay with her . . . forever. He knew then that he could take orders from her. She was strong. She was loving. She took his large head into her hands, bent down and kissed him above his eyes. "Good-bye, Solamen," she said. "We will miss you."

Then John carefully took the rope from the Centurion and walked out pulling Solamen gently with him. Solamen hesitated, but Jesus' mother placed her hand on his head and walked forward with him to the shade of a tree to which a large war animal was tethered. The animal snorted at Solamen and moved his rump and strong hooves in his direction. But the Centurion quieted the large animal with a pat and a whisper in his ear. The war animal held still while John attached the long rope holding Solamen to the animal skin seat atop his back. The Centurion mounted and clicked his tongue at the war animal. It moved slowly forward dragging Solamen over the dirt street.

John's voice came after them, choked with tears, and repeating over and over: "Go, go. The Lord be with you both."

CHAPTER XIX

Captivity

Solamen fought with the rope; pulling hard; shaking his head when the war animal paused; digging his straightened legs into the dirt road, a brake on the Centurion's mount. He strove for many miles to escape. He had seen many prisoners in a position like his. Except that the ropes were around their waists, not their necks. They had fallen many times, and sometimes the soldiers would take their large cutting metal pieces that they wore, and cut the rope on a downed prisoner. Then, just as the prisoner rose and started walking, they would use the same metal piece to pierce him. Nothing slowed them down. They stopped for no one. The wounded soldiers were put into the carts that rumbled over the dusty roads. And when the Centurion met up with his own pack, he put Solamen into one of those empty carts. First he tied the rope to the cart wheel. Then he went over to Solamen to pick him up. Solamen felt anger stirring inside. His eyes clouded. He wanted to harm the Centurion who was taking him from those he loved. But John had given him to this human. So instead of lashing out, he struggled until the Centurion lost his hold around his middle, and Solamen slid out of his grasp and onto the ground, rump first. He darted forth . . . until the rope stopped him with a jolt that made him lose his footing. Immediately the Centurion regained his hold, and leaning against the cart for support, grunting, he tossed him into the cart. There he sat. And then, as the group of soldiers moved on, he gnawed at the rope, now shortened and attached to the front of the cart.

He rode all day, feeling each bump in the road as the cart rolled forward. The Centurion rode the war animal and came to check on Solamen at intervals, hanging his arm over the side of the cart, talking to him in coaxing tones, setting before him a pan of water and morsels of meat. Not what Solamen wanted. He didn't touch any of it.

Farther and farther he went from Jesus. And his mother. And John, the youngest pack member. They all came into his mind as the cart rumbled on. He had to get back to them. How could he not protect Jesus' mother?

When the army of men stopped, Solamen heard their dinner preparations. He smelled a roasting field animal, and despite his unhappiness, his saliva began to gather in his mouth. The Centurion brought him a side piece, still somewhat uncooked, as the fire had not yet reached that depth from which it was torn. He also brought a fresh pan of water. He put both on the ground and untied the half-shredded rope from the cart, looping it through a cart wheel, and invited Solamen to jump down. He gave entreating clicks with his tongue and then sat next to the cart in the shade to eat his own dinner.

He stayed there though the sun disappeared behind the horizon and the moon slowly rose. Other soldiers came and spoke and laughed with him and stood on their toes for a glimpse of Solamen. As each one peered over the side of the cart Solamen felt his hackles rise. These were not like the Centurion. There was a difference in the way he carried himself, the way he spoke to others, the way he smelled, as strong from the heat as his pack members, but without their unease. Perhaps it was his carriage. He was more confident. Like a pack leader not needing to strut. Though he was a Roman leader, he emitted a touch of the warmth and assurance of Jesus' pack members, like John, like Jesus' mother. Solamen could feel no duplicity in him. He, unlike so many others, conquerors and conquered alike was not torn on the inside. He did not try to go two opposite ways at once. Like the ones who wore metal pieces had. Like the tight-skinned one. Like Taursus.

So not that night, but in the morning, Solamen jumped stiffly from the wagon while the soldiers were eating. The Centurion saw him and brought his army animal to the cart and fastened a new rope onto his animal skin seat and onto Solamen's collar. As the Centurion walked away, Solamen moved slowly from the cart and into the bushes to urinate. The rope was lax, and he was surprised that it did not hold him back. After he scratched beside his toilet spot, he walked away from the spot, stiff-legged, one step at a time, a long pause between each step. He was heading for a break. He scoped out the landscape. Where were the fewest soldiers? Where was there a quick path to a clump of trees? What about the Centurion? Obviously gone off somewhere to check on his army men. Good! With an enormous burst of energy which took the army animal at the other end of the rope off guard and sent it to its knees Solamen spurted . . . and felt himself thrown head over heels onto the ground. The rope had held. The army animal whinnied and stomped as it struggled back to its feet, angry at having been surprised. And Solamen, as if such actions were just a normal part of each day, shook himself and walked nonchalantly back to the wagon and drank the water and ate of the roasted flying animal. Then he lay down. When the Centurion returned, Solamen could feel through the ground the movements of the many soldiers preparing to march again. He jumped into the wagon without an order. He would not look at the Centurion.

Of course he remembered his old army days as he traveled with this group. Then he had been free to roam, to chase and terrify. The images came back to him: the male human he had killed for a fish; the young ones he had killed just for fun. He had been like the worst of the soldiers. Wicked and disgusting. He enjoyed their company, but never liked any of them. They were simply joined through their common meanness. He always knew that at any moment they could have turned on him, on each other. He was always ready to turn as well.

As the army moved on Solamen became more accustomed to his captivity. Now he ran beside the cart in the morning, rode the cart in the heat of the afternoon, and went back to walking in the evening. When he was tethered to the army animal, he tested the rope, but gingerly. He had learned his lesson. The Centurion treated him like royalty. The Centurion always received the choice pieces of the meat and vegetables as was his due because of his rank; now he took double portions and gave the larger to Solamen. Still Solamen refused to look at him. Even when he took Solamen's large head into both his hands and spoke kindly to him. Solamen shifted his gaze to the side and ignored him as much as possible, simply waiting for another chance to bolt.

One morning the smell of salt told Solamen that the army was near a large sprawl of water. When they came to the place with floating nests, they stopped and reorganized. All of the soldiers walked up planks that breached the distance from the landing to the floating nests. The Centurion waited until last. Then he came to where Solamen sat in the shade. He took a second rope and fastened it to Solamen's collar. He summoned another soldier and handed him one rope, taking the other for himself. He then unleashed the army animal from Solamen, wrapped ropes about its middle, and had it lifted aboard the floating nest.

Next he started up the plank pulling Solamen with him. At first Solamen resisted, but with two ropes attached he knew he had no chance of escape. So he conceded. Up the plank he went and into the hold of the ship. It was a place from which he could not escape. Only one upside down door. It smelled dank and sour from the barrels of drink. He found traces of human excrement and blood as he roamed from one spot to another. Old, musty ropes. Cast off hand bindings which smelled of other prisoners, humans who had been put where he was now. No windows. It was dark. He was more prepared for darkness than the humans who had been tethered where he was now. He needed less light than they to see. Besides, he knew in his bones when it was night, when it was day. He had his inner clock which told him the movement of the heavens. He didn't need the light and dark. Still he hated it here. He lay down reluctantly on the mat the Centurion had laid for him.

He felt the rocking and jerking as the floating nest left its moorings. The Centurion came to see him, struggling down the narrow rope steps to the bottom of the boat at least three times a day. At the last watch, for Solamen knew it was such (he remembered that the soldiers were assigned to guard in time watches all day and all night), the Centurion came down and sat on one of the barrels. He carried a burning fire on a stick which made all the objects around him, which Solamen had barely distinguished, clearly visible. He brought special treats which Solamen picked up gingerly from the floor. He would not take them from the Centurion's hand.

Once a day he opened the top door and urged Solamen to come forth. He tried. The rope steps were not only slippery under his feet, but they had spaces between them. He tried to place his feet upon each one, but his body was so bulky that he would slip off from his own weight. So the Centurion would go down to him, wrap ropes about his body and signal two others to lift him up to the floor above where the air was fresh and the sun warmed his coat. With those two ropes attached to the Centurion and another soldier he remained on the main deck of the nest for a few hours before being returned under the floor.

And thus, in that manner Solamen came back to the city with the amphitheater. When they lifted him for the last time from the place under the floor, he knew where he was. He knew. He had known that the Centurion was taking him away from those he wanted to be near. Now he knew the Centurion was taking him where he did not want to go. Where he never wanted to go again.

Once more the floating nest rocked and jerked and then settled into its own temporary nest. Solamen heard planks squeaking and protesting as they were trod by the footsteps of many men; then the cheers and screams of a welcoming crowd of conquering peoples. He shivered as the wind brought their scents, scents that he had smelled so often in the amphitheater.

Before he had time to ponder all the sounds and smells, the Centurion was standing above him on the floor of the floating nest. He came quickly down the rope pieces. He landed with a bounce and bumped into Solamen. "Sorry, old man," he joked as Solamen rocked sideways. For the last time he felt those ropes tightening about his middle, like a huge hand of fate, as he was lifted up. Two soldiers held his ropes.

The army animal was held on deck also. Pawing and snorting. Eager and happy. If he were loosed, he would not run away from the army, but to it. He was where he wanted to be. He gave Solamen a look of disdain. Flash back pictures roared through Solamen's brain. Taking down these proud animals in the amphitheater. Attacking the leg sinews. Avoiding the strong hooves. They were easy prey compared to the huge, heavy animals with horns and skinny tails with a handful of hairs at the end. Solamen glared angrily. Any animal would have the upper hand if the other was handicapped with ropes and guards.

The army marched through the town over the streets paved with large stone slabs. The Centurion rode first on the big army animal. Solamen walked reluctantly beside him. The conquering humans lined their path and threw large colorful objects at them. Solamen ducked at first. Then realizing that these were the soft puffs that crowned the field plants, he strode on. The army animal snorted blissfully, tossed its large head and pranced even more proudly, shifting its hind quarters back and forth so that Solamen had to be careful not to be stepped upon. They walked until they came to the huge round building with the open arches and the hollowed-out spaces for animals and humans underneath. They proceeded under the arch until they were back in the amphitheater.

At that point Solamen could no longer continue. His saliva dripped from his mouth. Visions of his last encounter here invaded his brain. He heard the screaming crowd urging him to kill. He felt nets upon him though there were none. He saw the wretched Taursus. He felt the other rope which had dangled him and spun him taking all his breath away. For the second time in his life he felt terror. First was the water test. Now this. He stopped and pulled back with all his strength. But the war animal had felt it coming, had sensed his fright. He was not going to have his triumph marred. So as Solamen resisted, the other one jerked him forward, causing the Centurion who was waving to the crowd, to pause and look to his rear. He urged him on. And so did the crowd. It began shouting: "On, on, on." It terrified him. He pulled backward to no avail. He dropped his body into the dust and let the war animal tug him forward.

In a special place in the stands, filled with many, many of the soft field blooms and pieces of waving colored cloth, a male human rose from his seat. He too yelled "on!" And a huge wave of silence went round the amphitheater. Out from under the stands ran an Editor. He ran to Solamen, whip in hand. But he didn't hit him. Instead, when he looked at him one on one, Solamen noted a change in his breathing. He dropped the whip, extended his arm sideways toward Solamen, turned to the male human who obviously led the many, many humans here today, and blurted out: "It's Auris Brevis! It's Daemon!"

Hearing that old name confused him. He rose to his feet and the important male human laughed and clapped. And soon the others clapped too. The Centurion showed by a weakening of his muscles that he was confused. Solamen smelled his sweat on his arms and on his chest under his metal plates. He stopped the war animal.

Solamen also felt the eagerness of the one who had called him Daemon. That one's chest rose in happiness. His feet, as he bowed to the important one, had trouble holding still. Finding Solamen utterly delighted him. Solamen worried about his intentions. He did not trust him. He may have been richly dressed, but he was a bad pack member with a load of troubles.

From the stands one voice, then two, then groups took up the chant: "DAEMON," "DAEMON," "DAEMON." The call grew so loud that it shook the stands. Solamen sensed all the life frustrations in the yelling and stomping pack: the hard labor with insufficient pay; the loneliness; the anger looking for a holding place; the thirst for dominance; the thirst for blood; the lack of love. He had been there. He had known it. He did not want to go back.

The important one allowed the shouting for a long time. Then he rose from his seat. Instant silence. A breathless silence. He motioned to the Centurion who dismounted. He walked over and stopped at the ditch full of water and the tall wall which separated the important one from the play in the amphitheater. At that point he bent his body in half in tribute. It was easy to see who was the pack leader here.

The important one leaned forward and spoke to the Centurion. He held a crown of leaves between his hands. The Centurion answered. He pointed to Solamen and slumped his own body until his back wore a hump. He put on an old look. He pointed to the unseen cages from which came yelps and growls indicating the kinds of animal fighters they held, shook his head, spread both hands toward the ground and again pointed to Solamen.

The important one put his hand up to his chin and rubbed it. Then looking at the crown in his hand, motioned the Centurion to come closer. From the way that he tossed the crown over the wall to the Centurion, Solamen knew it was no longer valuable to either human. In Solamen's memory the important one always set the circle upon a kneeling, conquering soldier. There was always a happy expectancy in the air. Today, though, the distracted Centurion caught it and plopped it unceremoniously upon his own head. Confused and obviously unhappy he backed up step by step until he was beside his war animal. That one snorted and pawed the ground until the important one gave another signal. The Editor ran out with a huge circle of blooms. He couldn't reach high enough to circle the war animal's head. So the Centurion, who had entered the amphitheater proudly and happily, now drained of all happiness, motioned the war animal to its knees. He took the crown of blooms from the Editor and plopped it over his shining, dark and proud head. The war animal quickly rose from its knees, snorted again and shook its head. He had his tribute. To him all was well.

It was a long afternoon. After watching a series of other humans stand and bow one by one to the important one, and some give speeches, Solamen hoped the important one would leave, exit the stands. He knew the humans in the stands would stay as long as the important one did. And that one did not seem eager to leave, though he showed with sharp barks his impatience with the speakers and caused them to quickly finish speaking. Actually no one wanted to leave. Anticipation swelled the air.

The Centurion, his horse, and Solamen were motioned to the sidelines where Solamen sat and witnessed the speakers and the slowly descending sun. The important one intended to stay a long time. Even though it was still light and even though it distracted from the speakers, he had some slaves come out with huge fire branches and put them into holders around the amphitheater which brought day again. Now the humans, who usually began shifting their bodies and wanting to leave the amphitheater, were still and expectant. Obviously they were waiting for something more exciting than the talks.

Solamen sneaked a look at the Centurion. He was more troubled than he had been at Jesus' mother's nest. He had taken off his head covering and his dark, curly hair was wet with water. The crown of blooms draped his neck. He stood leaning against his war animal, one arm slung over its rump. It patiently accepted his weight. It knew the order of command. Solamen was still attached to the animal skin seat.

CHAPTER XX

Courage

Solamen felt the excitement building in the stands and knew a contest was near. Why was the Centurion, unlike those honored ones Solamen remembered, not invited into the stands and into the important one's sitting place to watch it? Why were Solamen and the war animal not ushered into a safe place to wait for him at the close of the events? Why keep the three of them here on the sidelines ... they were going to put on a show for the important one? Unlike the war animal, Solamen had no illusions. He could feel the crowd's blood lust and now knew he was to be part of a hunt. Would he be hunter? Or hunted? What of the Centurion? What of the war horse? The Centurion did not look his way.

Two slaves pulled a young one from under the stands. She was dirty and even from a distance Solamen could smell that she had fouled her cage and then lain in it for more than a day. Her short covering was torn from one shoulder and slit on the other side so that part of her thin buttocks was exposed. Her hands were tied with ropes that cut into her wrists. Her feet were bare. Her head hair was matted. A large patch of it was missing on one side. She stumbled and whimpered as she was led out. Solamen knew that she was the weakest of the weak. She had not, nor could she now, offer any resistance to an attacker.

Solamen saw and felt the startled response of the Centurion. When he saw the young, pitiful human, he withdrew his arm from his war animal and shook his head. He looked at Solamen sitting next to him, but Solamen looked away.

The important one motioned them toward the girl who was being chained to a post in the center of the amphitheater. At the same time slaves carried out and quickly deposited potted, blooming plants and bushes. Solamen smelled the fresh soil on their roots. They had been dug from another area and contrasted with the trampled and stale blood aromas of the amphitheater floor. Yes, the aesthetics were being assembled for a hunt.

Solamen felt the Centurion's resistance.

"What has this person done?" he asked respectfully of the important one.

"Stole something or other," was the curt reply. "It doesn't matter. It will be an easy kill for Daemon. The others here remember him. They want to see him in action again. Then you can all go home. You have been on a long tour. I understand. A simple matter this. To please the crowd. Then you go home to a rest." He moved his shoulders grandly and including the crowd in his next gesture, he smiled. His largess was sealed by his grand: "I promise."

"How old is he?"

"It's not a he. It's a she," the important one retorted angrily. Then he shrieked: "Enough! Now DO it! Make Daemon kill!"

At that the crowd again took up the roar: "DAEMON, DAEMON, DAEMON."

The Centurion knelt down beside Solamen. He took that head, which refused to turn his way, into his strong hands.

"I promised I would protect you," he whispered. "When I took you away, I promised Jesus' mother that nothing bad would happen to you. I could have fulfilled that promise even if I had brought you with me, had I left you out of this amphitheater. If I had done that, you would now be sitting in my home. Far away from this madness. Fed by slaves and enjoying a beautiful courtyard with lush flowers and small trees. A beautiful retirement. Far from this poor, wretched girl. I am so sorry. I have been away on duty for many years. This is my first time in an amphitheater and all I had pictured of it was gladiators fighting each other, wild animal hunts, executions of hardened criminals, not this. She is but a child, not yet even budded into womanhood."

Solamen felt his distress. But he also felt something else. Integrity. This one's interior matched what he showed on the outside. He could also feel in the shift of the strong hands on his jowls that the Centurion had made a decision. Unlike so many army men when faced with death, he would not surrender. To obtain his own freedom he would not take the easy way out of this amphitheater. He would not attack this young one being tied to a pole. He would follow his inner directions. He would follow the way of John who refused to taunt Andrew; of Jesus' mother who hugged and fed Solamen, the unclean one; of Jesus who helped the weak ones and stood up to the ones with conflicting interiors even though it meant his own death. These all passed through his consciousness.

Solamen relaxed his head, stopped pulling against the hands of the Centurion. He turned his head and looked directly into the Centurion's eyes, into this man's soul, whose name he did not even know because he had not wanted to know it. All he had wanted this whole trip was to leave him, to get away and get back to Jesus and his mother. Now, as he focused on this man's interior, he found something of Jesus, his refusal to terrorize, to take advantage and to wantonly harm a weak one, despite the repercussions. He found there the wonderful strength of fellowship of those true followers of Jesus. Together, here in this amphitheater among all the screaming watchers with their disjointed interiors, the dog and the Centurion alone held a good common cause.

Meeting those gold, luminous orbs which had always evaded him, the Centurion started. His battle-ready posture relaxed, his eyes reflected that canine glow. His voice was filled with emotion: "Thank you for forgiving me," he said, "and for accepting me as your leader. Your free acceptance means more to me than all the kneeling and scraping obedience of those I have conquered. And there have been many: soldiers, political leaders, priests, even one king who knelt before me and offered his sword. Yet none gave me the happiness you give me today.

"I would so much like to take you home with me and share with you a place of peace."

Placing his paw on the Centurion's arm Solamen promised his fealty. The Centurion had a new follower, not as a conscript as were his many others, but as a volunteer. The Centurion returned the dog's pledge by placing his own sweaty hand upon that huge black paw.

Battle trumpets blared an interruption. Conscious again of their surroundings, Solamen and the Centurion were back in the amphitheater. The young human at the pole was sniffling and moaning. Terrified eyes watched Solamen. The fighter dogs were snarling in their cages, pawing for release. The army animal was bouncing on all fours. The important one was yelling and throwing his arms up. It was not good. The Centurion released Solamen. Both stood. The important one was yelling an order at them. It wasn't "free dog," but Solamen caught that meaning anyway.

The Centurion knelt again beside him. Slowly he put his hands on Solamen's neck. As he did, he turned Solamen's head away from himself and pointed it toward a narrow pathway from the amphitheater. It was a hot day and someone had left open the outside doorway to the evening breeze. An escape route. Solamen saw it. But he too had made a decision. He would only escape with the pack leader, not like the curs who turned when the fight began. Right now he was where he wanted to be.

The Centurion rose again and stepped to the army animal. Solamen shook himself as the collar and lead were released, first from the animal skin seat atop the bloom-headed army animal, and then from around his own neck.

The terrified human increased her screams, as much breath as she had. It was coming in gasps. Flash back to other like situations. How different he had once been. How he had enjoyed his dominance. How he had despised such creatures as this girl, how he had enjoyed terrifying them. How delicious a young one's flesh. The humans in the stands were as blood thirsty as he had been. Back then he had sensed their disjointed, even broken interiors, but he had been no better. Then he had not yet met John and Jesus and Mary, or even the Centurion. So he had been willing to take tribute from anyone.

The crowd began a heavy chant: "DAEMON," "DAEMON," "DAEMON." He couldn't tell from this distance if their eyes sparked green. But the encouragement amazed him. It was the strongest tribute he ever heard in this amphitheater. He was important today. The crowd was for him. He knew they wanted him to destroy this little one. Memories of his past kept flowing through his brain: the fisherman he had taken down, the woman misused by the army men in her own nest. He had missed his chance to maim and kill her because the soldiers were only interested in their own evil pleasure. Exactly why was he such a favorite of this crowd?

Because his preliminaries were the best. The soldiers would tie a young male human to a post. Sometimes they would give him a wooden, useless sword. When they let Solamen out alone, he would canter to the site. First he would circle behind the victim. He knew that with the human's limited field of vision, an attacker coming from behind him would be particularly terrifying. Next he would go to the front and walk stiffly up to and into the circle animals usually protected for themselves. Their private space. He gave this one no private space but filled it instead with his massive body. Then, reaching down to a leg that had missed being scrunched back, he would begin his sniffing. He started at the foot with a soft touch and an occasional drool as he proceeded up the leg. Usually the human would pull up his legs and expose his knees high to cover his private parts. But when he finished sniffing his way over the knee and down the groin, he would take his massive head, force it between the victim's knees and sniff his private parts, his stomach and up to his shoulders. At that point, if the human remained frozen, he would continue over each eye, each ear and his mouth where he would deliberately exhale.

Before the victim expired of fright like one of the young field animals, he would attack. Eyes flashing, growling, his strong back feet scraping, tail low and slowly drifting right to left he would rip into whatever part of the body seemed most vulnerable.

He would not kill right away. Instead he would maim with a rhythm to match the pulse of the crowd. His timing was exquisite. No other fighter dog had this skill. At each new scream of the crowd, he would rush in and slash a new wound into the victim, then pause with bloody foaming mouth as the victim pulled away so hard that the chains that held him bit into his wrists and drew blood. Solamen would lick off all the blood trickling from those self-inflicted injuries before he rushed for another bite.

But that was a long time ago. Before he knew Jesus. He would not do that now. He knew that Jesus would not bind or terrorize anyone. Instead, he welcomed and cured the weak of the crowd, their blindness, lameness and skin covered in sores. When he did, Solamen could also feel a change in so many of the crowd who had no outside weakness. Often he could feel their interiors heal as they stood before Jesus. Jesus was the greatest pack leader of all. He had a tremendous number of true followers as well as his tight little pack. No way would he have taken down this most vulnerable of creatures, no matter the consequences. Neither would Solamen.

So he stood stiff-legged after his release from the collar. He didn't take the escape route from the arena. Instead, with an aloofness befitting a prince he sat next to the Centurion and coolly watched the crowd.

The important human stood again. The others quieted instantly – silence before a storm.

The important human waved at the Centurion. He motioned him to hit Solamen and drive him toward the young one.

Instead the Centurion leaned down and told Solamen he was on his own. "I will not order you to kill." Solamen understood.

Next the important one motioned the Centurion again to the wall beneath him. From under his coverings, heavy with metal pieces like the important ones of the conquered peoples, he took an animal piece with a handle. It had straps with little metal tips. He tossed it to the Centurion who caught it and fingered it thoughtfully. The important one pointed to Solamen and made a sharp, downward motion which made Solamen growl softly. He understood: the important one wanted the Centurion to beat him and drive him toward the young, groveling human. He remembered how in this very amphitheater they used to beat the half-starved animals into fighting. He himself had never had to be goaded into a fight. He had lived for the charging, the feinting, the slashing, all of that. Against the defenseless. And against those who could slash back . . . but never had a chance, no matter how well they fought, to leave the amphitheater. Sometimes the human fighters burdened with many scars from many fights, left the amphitheater at the pleasure of the important one. Never to have to return. Not any animal he remembered had left.

Today the Centurion ruined both their chances to leave. In the soft uneven glow from the branched lights that grew brighter as the sky over the amphitheater darkened the Centurion walked backwards over to Solamen. He bent his body toward the important one though his heel felt for Solamen. Then with a downward sweep of the whip he had been given, with a fierce wallop, he hit the ground and dropped the whip into the dust. It lay but a short moment alone before it was joined in rejection by the Centurion's crown of leaves.

"Fool," the word was shouted from the side lines. The soft gasp of the entire crowd of humans could not drown it out. The Editor, trembling from head to foot continued: "All the dog had to do was one easy take-down. All of us, you, the dog, me, your horse. All of us would have received our freedom. Go home. Live it out. Now look what you have done! You have challenged our sacred emperor."

Solamen prepared for battle. Would they take on all the humans? Or all the fighter dogs? Anything was possible when the important one scrunched up his face and stiffened all his limbs. He did appear bigger. But this time he didn't seem powerful. Solamen sensed that his interior and exterior were totally conflicted. He could order a kill. He could not order respect. Nothing he could do would change Solamen back to the Daemon he had been. He braced himself on all fours. He waited for the Centurion's command.

The people were silent. Solamen sensed their indecision. They were no longer yelling "Daemon." They were not thumbing down for a kill of the young one. What did they want? Blood. Just blood, so that they could be pumped up and return to their unhappy lives knowing that someone else was worse off than they.

Red-faced and cunning as a vandal, the important one spoke one last time to the Centurion: "Will you deny your Emperor? Will you throw away twenty years of service? All the spoils of conquest? All the honors? Will you see your magnificent mount ripped to shreds here before you? Will you throw away all for the sake of this groveling human?" His voice cracked in anger: "Your dog will also be shredded into bloody rags upon this amphitheater floor. And you yourself will do no better. You will be part of the spoils of this war with me that you have chosen!"

The army mount tossed his head and whinnied at the slow pace of things; he was still totally unaware of his own danger. The Editor shrank to the smallest size he could, hugging the wall and slinking backwards to the place under the stands. The Centurion stood tall, but his uncovered head dripped water and his glands emitted battle smells. He wound his hand into the fur on Solamen's neck and whispered so that Solamen was the only one in the amphitheater who could hear:

"Lord Jesus, help me to be faithful as this beast." It was their last touching.

To the emperor he replied: "Your highness, I have fought for the empire for twenty years. All those years spent away from my home. Through all my campaigns. Through all the contests. Through all the intrigue of

216

foreigners I obeyed your laws. Now you say I will die here before you if I do not ask my dog to torture and kill. I cannot ask that of him. But even if I asked him, he would not do it. He has changed. He is no longer a Daemon. As for what this disobedience will cost me: all that I can say is: 'Some trust in horses, some trust in chariots; I trust in the name of the Lord,' of my Lord, Jesus."

With that he walked to one side of the young one, drawing her up to her feet. He motioned Solamen to the other side of her. From his position next to her Solamen gently supported her slumping body. Watching him the crowd shifted, its anger building until it was totally allied with the emperor and all thumbs were pointing down at Solamen with a raucous and loud call for his death.

Four fighter dogs took down the handsome army animal who was unaware of his danger until the last moment. Then came the Editor, dragged screaming from under the stands for the amusement and delight of the crowd. After his disposal the emperor pointed to the young one, but Solamen and the Centurion protected her, and four fighter dogs soon lay bloodied and dead in the dust.

The young one stood tall after that. She reached out and clenched the skin of Solamen's neck, now bloody from the fighter dog onslaught. Solamen, who once had to smother his growling when a female human approached him because he so scorned weakness, did not shrink from her touch. Instead he shifted his strong right shoulder under her arm to support her small, starving body. And she pushed gratefully back into him and smiled.

The emperor grew even angrier and the crowd with him. Under a very dark sky, split with the circles of light from the branches, he stood. Waving both hands toward the tunnels under the amphitheater he signaled for the release at once of all the remaining fighter dogs. There were twenty-five.

But soon it no longer mattered. Solamen was bleeding profusely, his life ebbing away. Peace flooded his being as his memory drummed the message of the pack urging him through the water to Jesus: "Hurrah" "Hurrah."

When fourteen dead fighter dogs lay strewn about, as well as five lifeless mounds of prey, no more taunts came from the assembled crowd. The important one yelled and clapped, but no one joined him in celebration. After the killings all in the crowd left silently. To these Romans courage was a virtue.

HUMAN'S VIEW OF SAME EVENTS

QUESTIONS FOR DISCUSSION

1. Daemon was raised with only abuse to direct his actions. How deeply ingrained is this training, and what are the influences which turn him to a better way?

2. The animal fights in the Roman coliseum were staged to entertain the crowd. How do they differ from entertainment for large audiences today? Is there any arena still relying on bloodshed and death? Are bull fights still held? What about back-alley dog fights? Is any of this legal anywhere?

3. According to the story, was John in real danger from Daemon? Was Jesus? Why do you think that Jesus never followed after John's captors? Why did Daemon not follow?

4. Why was John conflicted in his relationship with Daemon? Why did he not allow Daemon closer? Why did he not chase him away? How did the other characters view Daemon? Were any influenced by Jesus' outlook? By their religious practices? By the same kind of attraction that we have to these creatures?

5. Why do you think Matthew was relieved of his control of the money for the group? What was his occupation before he met Jesus?

6. Daemon saw many things from a perspective that differed from that of the humans about him. Can you name some of these?

7. What is the significance of the rescue of the staff of John? What might the staff represent?

8. What is the significance of the three falls Daemon had while carrying the staff?

9. What was the crowd's final assessment of Daemon?

10. Are you, as a reader, saddened by the books conclusion? Why? Or why not?

11. Like Daemon, do humans need a connection, a pack, as it were? Why is it difficult to turn from the praise of one's peers?

SELECTED REFERENCES

Canine history:

"Battlefield Dogs."
http://EzeneArticles.com/?expert=Geoffrey_English (n.d.)

"Dogs that changed the world." September, 2008.
http: //www.pbs.org/wnet/natural episodes/dogs that
changed the world.html.

"History and Origin of the Molosser Breeds." http:
//www.bulldog information.com/molossus-mastiff-
breeds-history.html (n.d.)

"Self Domestication." http://en.wikipedia.org/wiki/ self-
domestication. (n.d.)

Thurston, Mary Elizabeth: The Lost History of the Canine
Race. Kansas City, Missouri: Andrews Mcmeel, October,
1996.

Sources for dog knowledge:

Bodo, Murray. Francis, the journey and the dream.
Cincinnati, Ohio: Saint Anthony Messenger Press, 1988.

Coppinger, Raymond. Dogs: A new understanding of
canine origin, behavior and evolution. Chicago, Illinois:
Simon and Schuster, 2001.

Dodman, Nicholas H. Dogs Behaving Badly. New York, New York: Bantam Books, 1999.

Fox, Michael W. Dog Body, Dog Mind. Guilford, Connecticut: Lyons Press, 2007.

Grandin, Temple and Johnson, Catherine. Animals in Translation, Interpretations of Animal Behavior. Orlando, Florida: Harcourt, Inc., First Harvest Edition, 2006. (Using the Mysteries of Autism to Decode Animal Behavior.)

Horowitz, Alexandra. Inside of a Dog – What Dogs See, Smell, and Know. New York, New York: Scribner, Division of Simon and Schuster, 2009.

Kerasote, Ted. Merle's Door. Lessons from a Freethinking Dog. Orlando, Florida: Harcourt, Inc., First Harvest Edition, 2007.

Information on early Christian era:

Committee on Translations of the United Bible Societies. Fauna and Flora of the Bible. New York, New York: United Bible Societies, 2nd edition, 1980.

Crossan, John Dominic and Reed, Jonathan L. Excavating Jesus Beneath the Stones, Behind the Texts. New York, New York: Harper Collins, 2001.

Elwell, Walter A. Baker Encyclopedia of the Bible. Michigan: Baker Book House, 1988.

Fink, John F. Jesus in the Gospels. Minnesota: St. Paul's Press, 2000.

Losch, Richard R. The Uttermost Part of the Earth. Grand Rapids, Michigan: Eerdmans Publishing, 2005.

Nardo, Don. A Roman Gladiator. San Diego, California: Lucent Books, 2004.

The New American Bible, St. Joseph Edition, Copyright 1970 and licensed by the Confraternity of Christian Doctrine New York, New York: Catholic Book Publishing Company, 1970.

Ray, Steve and Janet. Footprints of God, Pilgrimage to the Holy Land. 2011.

Ricci, Carla. Mary Magdalene and Many Others. Minneapolis, Minnesota: Fortress Press, 1994 (translated from Italian by Paul Burns, originally published in Italy, 1991 M. D'Auria, Editore: Naples, under the title Maria di Magdala e le Moltre Altre, 1991).

Source for reaction to healing, concerning energy frequencies and blockage in the human body:

Namburripad, Devi S. Say Goodbye to Illness, NAET. Buena Park, Calilfornia: Delta Publishing, 3rd edition 2002